JOHN PEARSON has spent the best part of his life as a youth mentor, with a passion for storytelling and revealing the truth. In his writing we notice that reality is not always what we first imagine it to be. Then, as we look deeper and experience the magic, we begin to expect the unexpected.

Timmy Flea – The Inner Circle

By John Pearson

Dedication

The writing of Timmy Flea is dedicated to My grandchildren. May they grow up to become warriors and Heroes in whatever the universe draws them to be.

I am also grateful to Daniel Blackham, for his illustrations. Andrew Grant, cover design and portrait.
JV Publishing for their editing. Family and friends for their support, and fellow writers for their encouragement and advice

Myth & Truth

It was 1931, and a conversation at Magdalen College Oxford between J.R.R. Tolkien, C.S. Lewis, and Hugo Dyson. The content was on whether truth exists within a myth. Lewis declared that myths were lies and therefore worthless, even though they *'breathed through silver'*. Tolkien went away and wrote, in defence, a poem called **Mythopoeia** (Mythmaker) – an encouragement to all creative writers. Two paragraphs are included here:

> You look at trees and label them just so,
> (for trees are 'trees', and growing is 'to grow');
> you walk the earth and tread with solemn pace
> one of the many minor globes of Space:
> a star's a star, some matter in a ball
> compelled to courses mathematical
> amid the regimented, cold, inane,
> where destined atoms are each moment slain.
> Man, Sub-creator, the refracted light
> through whom is splintered from a single White
> to many hues, and endlessly combined
> in living shapes that move from mind to mind.
> Though all the crannies of the world we filled
> with Elves and Goblins, though we dared to build
> Gods and their houses out of dark and light,
> and sowed the seed of dragons, 'twas our right
> (used or misused). The right has not decayed.
> We make still by the law in which we're made.

Tolkien

Introduction

Timmy, just fourteen years old takes an unexpected holiday and a mysterious adventure begins. The stone circle had been a safe place for Timmy, but when the stones begin to crumble, he discovers an ominous prophecy – The collapse of time!

The story of this emerging warrior takes us from 1980 to 2015, encountering sinister magic, a dragon, a wizard, and a secret cavern. An unusual relationship is struck, and his new friend shares valuable insights into nature, legend, the unknown of this world and beyond.

If anyone should decide to create a man, it would be unwise to disregard the boy. Within a boy, everything is much bigger. How else can he gain a competitive edge? Unspoilt, animated, opinionated, intuitive, with eyes of wonder. A cocktail of inquisitive mischief and imaginings can bring about a belief beyond what we can see.

There is a likelihood of steady growth or firework explosions in equal measure. He tries to be independent, though needing approval. Often bossy, selfish with an ability to make excuses. Yet, a call to be a warrior – to fight dragons and to become the hero. Living moment to moment, fearful of change and incredibly lonely. Above all, a boy questions and needs to know why. True magic is woven at many stages and continues to play a part if we could open our eyes to see it.

Our story begins in the year 1980.

Events

1980
An unexpected holiday
The cottage
Adventure begins
The waterfall
That crow
Inner circle
Halvor the wizard
A Murder mystery
Abandoned house
Hidden treasure
Lost in the river
Playing cards
Thunder and lightning
The Universe
A dark secret
Going home

1985
Peter
Circle of tears
Secret cavern
The dark cave
Setting things right

1991
Grandma
Inheritance
The Dragon

2002
Hearts Clubs Diamonds Spades

2005–12
Letting go

2015
Origen
New roots

An Unexpected Holiday

People were shouting and cheering, and rain clouds were gathering as Timmy Flea stepped up to the line. It was the end of term and the school sports day. His mum was there watching, and that morning she said, 'You can only do your best, Timmy.' There were seconds before the Starter would fire the pistol. Each second beat slowly in his chest. Timmy knew nothing of adrenaline, he just wanted it to be over with as quickly as possible. The finish line was only a hundred yards away. Timmy felt more scared than nervous, and his legs began to shake. BANG! He shot off like an arrow from a bow. He only had one thing in sight, and that was the end.

It seemed there was one thing he was good at. Running. He never intended to win, but crossing the line first meant he would have to go onto the stage and collect his prize. Another scary ordeal, though this was nothing compared to events yet to come.

So, you may wonder who Timmy Flea is, and why the strange name. He had been christened Timothy Walker, and when he was incredibly young, he mispronounced Timothy as Timmy Flea, which his mother continued to call him. The pseudonym stuck, and even his friends at school called him this. Timmy was quite proud of what he had created though he wondered if it still suited him as he had just turned fourteen. He had mixed feelings about his choice, for, at school, the phrase brought a dash of teasing, but on the other hand, it gave him a sense of importance, an identity. He often wished he had a simple name like his good friend Peter.

Timmy regarded himself as different from other boys, while his mother would say he was unique. As far as he could see, his thoughts and imaginings were quite different, even a little strange. He often struggled to make sense of life's situations, and the words silly and stupid affected him. There were no special labels that could be attached to him. He was just Timmy Flea.

It was mid-autumn and a half-term holiday. His grandmother had sent word to her daughter, asking if she would go and look after her. His grandma had not been well for a while and needed bed rest to fully recover.

"Oh, Mum, do I have to go?" Timmy said, "I am old enough to look after myself now."

"No," his mum said. "You're coming with me. I'm sure there will be plenty to do. I remember when I was a little girl…" He didn't listen to any more of his mum's story as he had heard it so often. Seeing only a long boring week ahead of him, he was not swayed by his mum's words. He also knew there was no sense in protesting as she had made her mind up.

The family home was a place wrapped in love, but his mum was down-to-earth and sometimes came over as not caring. Timmy's dad worked hard, but at home, you would often hear him in fits of laughter that they could not help joining in. Timmy was sad to be leaving his dad and best friend, Peter, behind, but it was only a week and things would be back to normal. Or would they?

His grandma, like his mum in her ways, lived in a small village called New Standing. It would be a two-hour train journey from the busy city to the quiet countryside, the train taking them as far as the nearby town. Timmy's mum was flapping about getting to the station on time, finding the correct train, and checking that they hadn't forgotten anything. She gave a long sigh of relief as she settled into her seat. "Here we are then," she said, a phrase she would often use.

By choosing a window seat, Timmy could watch the world go by. He also liked playing people games, guessing who people might be and their jobs. He spotted several businesspeople and a large man he imagined to be a wrestler. Another man across from them looked suspicious, constantly moving things in his bag but never taking anything out. Timmy thought the man's glasses didn't suit him and decided he was a spy.

There was a scary moment when the train entered a tunnel. The sound suddenly changed to a lower, muffled drone, and though the lights were on inside the train, the outside was dark. Timmy held his breath, and butterflies stirred in his tummy. In less than half a minute, they were out in the light of day.

Plans for this week's school holiday had to be changed at the last minute, and Timmy felt he would be bored, though he had no clue about the extraordinary events that were going to happen. He had visited before, though as the cottage was too small for their family to have a sleepover, they had never stayed overnight. He was also excited about sleeping on a camp bed in the lounge.

Mrs Baker, a friend of Timmy's grandmother, met them at the station and drove them to Grandma's cottage, which was no more than ten minutes away. Mrs Baker must have had a first name, but Timmy had never heard it used. He thought names were strange labels, and Mrs Baker was in the same category as doctors and teachers – people who were accepted without first names. From the car window, he caught a glimpse of the Standing Stones perched on a small hill outside the village, so he knew he was close to Grandma's cottage.

"Mum, can I go to the stone circle when we get to Grandma's?"

"No, it will get dark soon, and that is no place to be at night."

"I could just run there and back," Timmy persisted.

"No, you will need to help me unpack, set up your bed, and you can tell Grandma all you have been doing at school."

Having the whole back seat to himself, he spread out and slumped with his arms folded and a glum face. He knew this week would be dull and couldn't see any hope of that changing.

Timmy was still only a boy and struggling to find his way. His extended family said he was like his dad and yet so much like his mum. This young boy had a sheltered childhood. He had a couple of friends he would spend time with, but overall, he was a solitary person who wouldn't say boo to a goose, fearful of his own shadow. Sometimes, mainly when he was on his own, he would wonder who he was and, more importantly, who he would become.

Timmy would admit there were many things he wouldn't try. Swimming, for one, or anything to do with water. He preferred to leave a light on at bedtime and was afraid of heights. It seemed to him that he would never achieve anything, but so long as he could get through, then surely that would be enough.

Arriving at Grandma's cottage, his mum remarked, "Well, here we are then."

"Stating the obvious," Timmy said.

"What?"

"No, nothing, Mum, it's just you – the parts that make you who you are. Who else could you be?"

The Inner Circle

Timmy

The Cottage

Grandma's cottage was oddly shaped, having had an extension fitted over thirty years ago. Dad said it was the house that Jack built. Timmy had no idea who Jack was but thought he was probably not the best of builders. Grandma enjoyed her garden and had kept it tidy until her recent illness. It was looking a little wild, having been left unattended. Her husband had died before Timmy was born, so Grandma had been on her own for a long time.

The cottage was on a bend opposite Castle Farm. It was a busy place considering it was a short distance from the village. Neighbours would often pop in, which people of the towns and cities wouldn't dream of doing unless invited. The teapot was the most used item, and the kitchen table was a place for listening and talking. If there was ever to be a village boardroom, it would be Grandma's kitchen.

Gossip was never spoken, for people were respected and valued. The focus would be on support and finding ways forward. Conversations would often end in laughter and a feeling of satisfaction.

Grandma was pleased to see them, though when she squeezed Timmy's hand, he could see she was not well. Mrs Baker put the kettle on for a cup of tea while Timmy and his mother brought in their cases and began to settle in. Timmy had brought his sketch pad, pencils, a reading book, and a bag of comics from home.

Strangely, this little cottage seemed to have more rooms than there was space for. They were small rooms with steps up and down, creaky floorboards, and even noisier hinges. A door in the corner of the living room opened onto a second narrow staircase. Two steps up and a turn to the left, up more steps and a turn to the right, two steps up and into what used to be a tiny bedroom. Timmy had not been exploring long when he found himself in this room. It smelt old and musty and all he could see were old boxes of books and oddments that had belonged to his grandad. Timmy had heard talk of the room being cleared, but Grandma wanted it left as it was. The only window was a skylight in the roof, and by standing on a box, Timmy could see down the field to the wood and the hills beyond.

He found various practical and educational books with over half of them about birds. There were notebooks, too, with sketches of birds sitting and in flight, each one signed with the initials TB, Ted Bell. He must have been pleased with his work. Timmy was impressed as he didn't know his grandad could draw, but there were many things he didn't know about him.

An old, well-used walking stick was hanging on a hook behind the door. Gazing long and hard at the head of the stick, Timmy spotted a carved face with a long beard and deep eyes looking back at him. Perhaps it was a wizard? Words had been carved in a spiral down the stick, and as Timmy ran his fingers over them, he read, 'Hold on to what you have.' As he held the stick, a loud flapping noise made him jump, almost out of his skin. Spinning round, he saw an old crow at the window. Heart racing, he shouted at it, and it flew away.

Timmy's mother came up the stairs. "What's all the noise about? What are you up to?"

"I was scared by the crow at the window," he told her. "This stick is amazing. Can I borrow it?"

Her automatic response was, "No!" She was more interested in collecting the camp bed and chasing him back down the stairs. Timmy could not see how he would be comfortable on a piece of canvas and lumps of wood. He carried the stick with him, determined to ask Grandma if he could take it on a walk the next day.

There was a knock at the door, and an old, slightly built man stepped inside. Timmy remembered him as Uncle Bill, though there was no family connection. He also remembered him being a gardener. He studied Uncle Bill's smiling face, his impressive moustache waxed at both ends, looking long and stiff enough to withstand any wind.

"It's only me, Grandma. I'm just checking in to see how you are." It seemed strange he should address her in this manner, for they must be around the same age, but most people around here described her as such.

Bill was passionate about gardening, particularly gooseberries. He knew a lot about soil and how it supplied food for growing plants, and, that plants grew best in certain soil types in various places. Timmy remembered times as a young boy in the garden with Uncle Bill.

'It's just the way things are,' Uncle Bill would say. 'And so long as we work with the rules of nature, we get the best results. Life follows the same simple rule. Grow where you are planted, find the things you do best and most of all, have fun.'

Timmy didn't always know how to take some things Uncle Bill said. Was he serious? Did he mean that, or was he joking? Poor Timmy was trying to learn how to read people and finding it difficult. Like when Uncle Bill told him that, 'A seed had to be planted the right way up, so the roots grew down, and the stem grew up towards the sky.' Timmy didn't know how that worked but was sure there must be something in the seeds programming that dealt with those sorts of things.

"What can you tell me about the standing stones,

Uncle Bill?"

"Oh, they were dancing ladies that were turned to stone. Each one has a name, and if they ever crumble and fall, it is said, all time will collapse." Well, that was about what Timmy expected. "I was up there last week," Uncle Bill continued, "and I thought the stones looked tired."

"I guess they are very old," Timmy added, not wanting to think about the end of time and what might happen after that.

"Your grandad and I would play up there when we were children. He won a medal in the war, you know." Turning to Grandma, he said, "I'll not stop. I see you've got company. I might pop by later in the week. Nice to see you all." And with that, he was gone. Through the window, Timmy caught a glimpse of Bill as he paused to light his pipe, and then he heard the click of the garden gate.

Timmy asked his grandma about the War medal and discovered that Edward (Ted) Bell had been awarded a medal of valour during the Second World War. He was going to the aid of three comrades who were under fire and had run out of ammunition. Ted carried the necessary equipment, despite coming under attack from the enemy. After thirty minutes of intense fire, reinforcements arrived, and the position was held. Asked about the event, Ted would say anyone else would have done the same.

"Where's the medal now, Grandma?"

"I honestly don't know. I haven't laid eyes on it for years. Your grandad looked after such things. I am sure it's not in those boxes, as we packed all that."

Time passed, Mrs Baker left, and Grandma fell asleep. Timmy and his mother had their supper, and before he knew it, he was tucked up on the camp bed, which was surprisingly cosy. A bedtime strategy his dad had taught him was to think through the day's events. The packing and getting to the station, the train journey, Mrs Baker and Grandma, exploring the house, and long before he got to the scary crow, he was asleep.

Adventure Begins

During breakfast, the following day, Timmy's mum told him about paths in the wood, things to see, and places she had played as a young girl. Timmy reached for his toast and marmalade, thinking he would tease his mum. "Mum, are there any fairies, dragons or dark beasts in the wood?"

She smiled. "All those things are pure fantasy. They belong in storybooks." She lowered her head and looked straight at him. "However, there are mysteries to be solved just as there are stranger things within nature itself. You will see." This conversation did not go the way Timmy had planned, but now, he was on tenterhooks.

The letterbox rattled, and turning, Timmy caught sight of the postman through the window. His mum headed to the door. There was only one envelope. "I'll take it straight up to Grandma," she said. Returning to the kitchen, she announced, "That was nice. It was a get-well card from Cousin Jenny."

"Your cousin?" Timmy asked, "Do I know her?"

"No, Jenny is Grandma's cousin. You have never met her," his mum continued. "She's lived in Hastings for many years, moving there after Oxford. She's a journalist for the newspapers and never married," his mum paused, "before you were born, I remember your dad and I went to visit her while we were on holiday there. She looks a lot like your grandma."

Timmy frowned. "There are so many things I don't know about my family. It's much bigger than I imagined." He had a sudden thought. "We should have a guidebook or a map with people and stories."

His mum sighed. "We do. We have a box of photos. When we get home, you and I should sit down, and I will tell you all I can remember and how they fit into our family tree."

The idea of a family as a tree intrigued Timmy, and he began to wonder about the different branches and roots and how they all spread out. The roots, he imagined, must be deep in the ground, holding the tree firm against the wind.

Timmy was under strict instructions to keep his visit short when he went to Grandma's room. "Hi, Grandma, I wondered if I could borrow the walking stick when I go out today."

She lifted herself and puffed up her pillow. "Oh, that blessed stick. Your grandad took it everywhere with him. I am sure he spoke more to that stick than he did to me." She laughed. "Of course, you can borrow it." Pointing her finger, she continued, "So long as you take good care of it and return it to the hook behind the door." Timmy smiled and promised he would.

Later that day, he set out on an adventure with his new-found stick, the leather strap wrapped around his wrist. It was only a short walk to the wood's edge, and he strode out excitedly. He'd been told to keep to the path, to keep an eye on the time, and to be back before four. His mum had packed him a bun, a couple of biscuits, and a bottle of juice, and told him to find the waterfall, rest there for a while and enjoy his pack-up before returning home. There would be other days to explore further.

The trees in the wood seemed so tall, and light streaming in between them cast sunbeams across the path. Timmy had not realised how many shades of green there were. Light and shadows moved with the breeze, birds chirped, and rustling leaves betrayed the presence of squirrels. Noisiest was a single crow, and Timmy wondered if this was the same one that had frightened him at the window. The air was full of countless smells, things were growing, and others were rotting away, which is all part of the necessary order of things. What more would this young boy discover that day?

The path meandered through the wood, revealing itself only in short stretches because the wood was trying to hide it with creeping grasses and ferns. Occasionally there was a view of fields beyond the wood and the sound of a tractor ploughing one of them. The noises of the city were far from Timmy's mind now, and he felt very much part of the countryside, surprised at how much there was to see. Every so often, he would stop to gaze around.

He took a left turn and headed out of the wood. The waterfall would have to wait as he was heading for the stone circle. Having been taken there by his dad when he was young, this was by far his favourite place. When visiting Grandma, they would often spend time walking around the outside, sitting in the centre, and hiding behind the stones.

It was so peaceful there. He sat against the largest stone – the Portal – and looked across to the next village. Little Standing, the oldest village in this area, took its name from these standing stones. Timmy wished he had brought his sketch pad, as this would make for a great picture. He had never regarded himself as an artist. It was all for fun, something to while away time. His drawings were for his eyes only, so nobody could criticise or tell him how they should be.

Timmy got to his feet and began to walk clockwise around the nine stones, weaving in and out as he went. Running his hand across the stones as he passed, he noticed the strange symbols chipped into the surface. One stone appeared to be crumbling, and flakes fell to the ground as he watched. But, of course, these stones were ancient. After a short while, he left the circle and headed back towards the woods.

Origen

The Waterfall

There was a cool breeze as he entered the woods. Timmy felt secure and content in these familiar surroundings. Things seemed so predictable, as if all of this was the most natural thing in the world. He'd heard the rushing waterfall for the last ten minutes, and now it came into sight. He stood, holding the stick in front of him, hands clasped around the head, chin resting on them and found this a most relaxing position to watch the continuous falling water. The sight and sound he found mesmerising.

Suddenly a voice called out his name, "*Timmy, don't be scared.*" But there was no one around. The voice came neither from behind or above him nor from the waterfall. Instead, it was coming from the stick.

He let go sharply, but the stick did not fall because the strap was around his wrist. He shook it in fright, but all was quiet. Had he imagined it? Slowly, he rested his hands back on the head of the stick. The next moment, he heard the voice say gently, "*I only wanted to say hi. Please do not be scared. I was a friend of your grandad.*" The stick was speaking to him, and this was crazy. He wanted to run away as fast as his legs would carry him, but most of all, he wanted to know how this could happen.

Timmy took a deep breath and blurted out many questions. Finally, the stick suggested that he find a comfortable spot to sit and keep the stick under his arm. "*So long as you hold me, we can talk to each other,*" the voice explained.

Soon they were sitting comfortably, chatting away as if they had known each other forever. How could this be, the curious young boy wondered, was he dreaming? Did Grandad carve the stick, and when did it begin to speak? Can any stick speak? "Do you have a name?" Timmy asked.

Knowing everything that Timmy was thinking, the stick said, "*Your grandad found me among these woods, and we spoke long before he carved my head or at least something he imagined I might look like. I have no name,*" the stick continued, "*though as I came from an Ash tree, I could be called Ash. However, your grandad called me Origen, after a first-century philosopher. A name should describe who you are, don't you think? The word 'grandad' describes someone who has lived long and grown to love many times, a wise person with time and patience for others,*" the stick paused, waiting for a noisy crow to stop his chattering. "*I can only speak the truth, so if I don't know something, I will tell you I don't know.*"

Timmy spoke up, "I should like to call you Origen too. It feels right. I didn't know my grandad, but now I am beginning to learn more about him."

The stick explained that the words were not coming from him and that he had no voice as such. Timmy was hearing it in his mind, and in the same way, Origen could hear Timmy's words without him speaking out loud. Timmy felt safe with Origen but still found it more natural to talk out loud.

"*As to other sticks being able to speak,*" Origen continued, "*the whole of creation is constantly crying out to be heard, but man is too busy to hear. Listen to water rushing over stones, leaves falling from the trees, rustling in the breeze, branches creaking, and so much more if you only stop to listen to it. I am sure there are other sticks like me all over the world, but that's something we keep to ourselves. Most people would think the idea crazy.*"

Timmy was sure that he would never tell a soul and would like to keep Origen forever. "*Most things in life are to be shared, but some things are best kept to yourself,*" Origen said.

Timmy decided it was nature's choice to whom, how and when it speaks to us. As if all this were not strange enough, he noticed a figure approaching the waterfall. Even more strangely, he could see right through it. "Is it a ghost?" he asked.

"*I don't know what or who it is."* Origen said. *"I only know I don't believe in ghosts.*"

The movement of the figure looked familiar and stirred Timmy's curiosity. The words it spoke were short, "You're going to turn out just fine, Timmy Flea, just fine." Then it disappeared completely.

Timmy shook his head. "This has been the strangest of days. I will wake up at any minute and find it all a dream. Yet I know I am wide awake."

All was quiet for a moment, and then Origen replied, "*Most things happen for a reason. We just don't know it at the time.*"

Walking back to the cottage, Origen taught Timmy the names of the trees, grasses, ferns, moss, and fungi. It was like having a massive book in your head. Although this all seemed strange, there was something natural about his extraordinary experience.

"You sound like a teacher, but nothing like the ones we have at school," Timmy blurted out.

"*There are many ways to learn,*" Origen replied, "*but they all work best when linked to experiences.*"

"Did a magician make you?" Timmy asked.

"*I guess whoever made the universe and holds everything in place must be quite a magician. But as a teacher, I should point out that if knowledge such as this is used to gain power over another person, place, or thing, there will be dire consequences.*"

Arriving at Grandma's, Timmy was bursting to tell his mum about his adventure. So, without saying anything about Origen, he told her all the new things he had seen. The waterfall that was so loud, the trees' names and the noisy crow that had seemed to follow him all day. Timmy's mum suggested he wash his hands, as dinner would soon be ready. He didn't want to let go of Origen but did as he was told and put it back on the hook behind the door.

That evening Timmy asked Grandma about the standing stones. She told him about the generations of children that had played there.

"Who built the circle and why?" Timmy asked.

"Ah, that's a good question," Grandma said. "Nobody knows, but there are stories about ancient people and their beliefs. Some say it was for studying the stars, but they are just guessing." She finished her cup of tea and rested her back in the chair. "The problem is they didn't write anything down in a way we can read them."

"What do you mean, Grandma?"

"They didn't have books. In any case, paper would never last all this time. They did chip symbols into the stone, but again we can only guess what those mean."

"I saw those symbols today. I had never noticed them before. The stones seem to be crumbling too."

Grandma's eyes widened. "It is supposed to happen one day, but I didn't think I would live to see it."

"See what, Grandma?"

"A legend we heard as children says that when the stones begin to crumble and fall, all time will collapse. So, we supposed it was a big clock."

Mouth hanging open, Timmy drew in a long breath. "Is that true? But what happens when there is no time?

Will the world stop turning?"

Grandma laughed. "Oh, these are just stories. Those stones have stood for thousands of years and will be here long after we've gone. I am sure the crumbling is just weather damage."

It was now dark, and Grandma said she was tired, though she had enjoyed the company sitting in her chair for half an hour. It was time to put up the camp bed and settle for the night. But unfortunately, there was so much in Timmy's head that falling straight to sleep was unlikely.

The Inner Circle

That Crow

Timmy's mum woke early and started work in the kitchen, creating a wonderful smell of baking. "I'm making bread today," she announced. "Are you ready for some breakfast, Timmy?"

Timmy was always ready for food. "Yes, please." He sat at the table and poured out cereal into a bowl.

She stopped what she was doing. "I have been thinking you should not go poking into things you don't understand."

He knew she was referring to the stones. "But, Mum, how can we learn if we don't explore?" He took another spoonful of Cornflakes. "I was nearly three years old when men landed on the Moon. That was a big step forward."

"That's different," his mum said, "but there are things we should not dabble with."

Timmy didn't always listen to his mother's words. It was not that he was intentionally disobedient, just that he felt there were things he must explore, and besides, she would never explain why he couldn't, shouldn't, or mustn't.

Out walking with Origen that day, Timmy wondered about the crow. Was this the giant bird that scared him at the window? It certainly seemed to have been following him around ever since. He asked Origen what he thought.

"*Well*," Origen began, "*that isn't a crow at all. It is true that he is part of the crow family and prefers his own company. He is also regarded as a rather clever chap. Some do say he is like a Joker, a bit of a fool, but* that's just a game he plays. His proper name is Jackdaw, probably because he shouts Jack-Jack-Jack as he chatters in the trees. He's a jackdaw, not a crow – a friendly fellow and lives in a chimney at the old house."

Timmy's eyes followed the jackdaw as he circled them, jumping from branch to branch. Whatever was this bird up to? He was more curious than a cat. "I will call him Jack. I wish he'd come closer so I could see his face and feathers, but he's probably afraid, fearful of being captured and put in a cage. Not that I would do that."

"*He doesn't know that,*" Origen said.

"So, what can I do?" Timmy asked.

"*There's nothing you can do. Soft words and a smile, moving slowly and quietly, will not work. A poacher will do all those things. When you are sitting still, and your whole self is at peace, perhaps he will come to you.*"

"But how can I feel at peace when there are so many things to think about? My head never stops. Mum says I'm like a spinning top, and most of the time, it gets in the way of my thinking, which scares me."

"*Fear is important to us because it helps keep us safe. You must first overcome your fear, and that will help Jack not to feel afraid. It might help if you have a happy thought.*"

Timmy's happy thought was clear, and a smile came across his face. His daddy, coming home from work and a ride on his bicycle.

Origen continued, "*First, you need to slow down. You can do this by breathing in deeply and slowly, then out deeply and slowly. Listen to your breathing and hold that happy thought. Let go of the fear.*" Timmy let out a long breath.

"*There you go – that's peace.*"

"I can hear things I couldn't hear before," Timmy

said softly. At that moment, the jackdaw flew down silently and perched on a branch within two feet of Timmy's nose. They stared at each other for what seemed like an age. Timmy didn't move a muscle, noticing Jack's eyes were pale white and his feathers like silk. There was a feeling of kindness and understanding about Jack. As the bird rose into the air, Timmy felt the down draught from his wings – then he was gone, but Timmy knew that would not be the last he'd see of him.

A little later, Origen mentioned that people talk to their dogs too.

"Yes, but they don't expect a reply," Timmy said.

"*Perhaps we should learn to expect the unexpected then. I am certain there is more to discover than we can imagine.*"

Timmy held the stick in both hands and studied the carved face. A sharp knife had left marks like wrinkles. Suddenly Timmy jerked. "You winked, and your nose moved. I saw you."

"*No, that's impossible. I am no more than a stick that cannot move on its own accord,*" Origen replied. "*I am within the stick but not part of it. I am also within all the trees, plants and earth... even in the wind.*"

Timmy frowned. "You are also magic, and magic can make things move."

"*What you perceive as magic is natural to me. Your imagination wanted to see a facial expression, so that is what you saw. How easily the human mind can be fooled, and how quickly does it form strong beliefs.*"

Timmy's close encounter with Jack had inspired him to draw, so he sat down and took out his sketch pad. He thought of his grandad's sketches and wondered if he could match them for detail. He began with basic shapes, though not without a bit of rubbing out. His schoolteacher had often told him to start things off simply, then to let them grow, and to look for an extra something that described the picture. Timmy wondered how he could draw the wind beneath Jack's wings and found the fine pencils helpful. The sketch grew and grew until it covered half the page, and Timmy was surprised at how big the beak was. Pleased with his work, he put the pad in his pocket and headed towards the waterfall. There were three of them now. Origen, Jack, and Timmy – four if you include the wind.

Timmy had assumed that the sound of the waterfall was always the same, but today he heard a different tone and saw a log jammed at the side nearest to him. The diverted water gushing over the larger rocks was causing the swirling noise. Timmy was about to release the log and return the flow to its normal state, but Jack began to chatter in alarm as if sensing danger. Timmy stepped closer, grabbed a nearby stick and began poking the log. This was not working, so he placed the stick under a rock to gain leverage. He leaned heavily on the stick and knew something had to give. The stick snapped, the log shifted its position, and the water pressure took it over the waterfall. Timmy smiled as he watched the log float gently on its way. It was so satisfying, and the waterfall's sound had lost its distress.

The Inner Circle

Jackdaw

Inner Circle

Their walk today took them back to the stone circle. Timmy meandered around the stones in wonder and amazement, as people must have done for thousands of years. "It is said that a stone circle is similar to a church, big and bold, a place where people meet for ritual. If these portal stones formed the circle entrance, you would imagine an outside fence or walls. Otherwise, people would walk in from any direction." Timmy carried Origen around the perimeter as if on a guided tour, relating details his dad had told him.

"*Stone circles date back three thousand years,*" Origen replied. "*It is likely that it was a temple, a place to make offerings to a god, or many gods. It's a place of atonement.*"

"That's a word I don't understand," Timmy said as he rested against one of the smaller stones.

"*The word atone literally means something agreed – at-one. Finding a way to bring things back to how they should be. People still believe that if something goes wrong, then something must be done, be paid for, to put it right.*"

"Like a sacrifice?"

"*Yes, that often happened. A sacrifice or payment would be offered to ensure clear weather for the crops and fertility for the animals. This was basic survival for the people of that time, their belief in gods and the elements supported this.*"

Timmy looked around and said, "We don't have sacrifice or atonement anymore, so is that why things go wrong?"

There was a long pause before Origen answered, "*In one way, we do not sacrifice as these people did. However, the need for atonement, to put things right, is still there. A person imprisoned for wrongdoing as a payback for their crime. Even as children, if there is something we want, we often say, 'Please, I will be good'.*"

Timmy wanted to get to the heart of this puzzle. "So, a payment, an offering to the gods – does it work? Is there any point to it?"

"*Yes and no,*" Origen said. "*I don't believe there is anything we can offer by sacrifice that is sufficient for mankind's wrongdoing. We want to change things because, throughout history, the world has been in a mess, which is not how it was intended. I think in the days when this was built, people had the right idea. They went to the centre of the circle, though they may not have realised that, caught up in rituals as they were. We need to enter the circle, with or without walls, through the portal stones – to leave outside the things we do not need, to approach the centre with intent so that our inner self might change. If we change for the better, surely better things will happen?*"

There was a long silence as this sank in. Timmy was the first to speak, "Suddenly, I need to say sorry for so many things."

"*That's good, Timmy. Forgiveness is part of the atonement. Saying sorry with all our hearts is the biggest part of the atonement. There are nine stones in this circle, and this is significant. Nine is a magical number associated with transformation, wholeness, and becoming one. People, nature, and the universe are all one. Everything works so much better when we recognise this oneness.*"

Leaving the circle today, Timmy sensed a change. Something of it had become part of him, and he felt special. Things were coming together, though making practical sense of it all was still beyond him. He decided not to think too hard as it made his head spin and he just needed to let it be for now.

That evening the sketchbook came out again as Timmy began to create an image of the ancient stones. This time he added figures going in and coming out of the circle. There were no walls. The people knew where they should go. It was all part of the ritual. There was a centre stone of offering and smoke was rising in the still air. His mum was impressed and suggested he framed his pictures.

"No, I prefer them in this book where I can look at them. It also keeps them in the right order."

She shrugged and went to the kitchen to prepare some supper. "What else have you been up to today?" she called to him.

His usual answer came back, "Oh, not much."

"I thought you might be bored with country life and having nobody to play with."

"Oh no, there's lots to explore each day, and it's still only Monday."

"I was worried you might be afraid to go out on your own." Her little boy was growing up and making choices. Parents can often miss this part of their children's growth, being too busy and secretly trying to keep them as small children.

They all slept soundly that night. Timmy's dreams took him back to the flat stone in the centre of the circle. In the dream, he laid down treasured items and toys he no longer played with but would never be parted from. It was as if space had to be made for something new that was coming. He was left with a puzzle. What will happen next?

Then the dream woke him, and he wanted to go and get Origen to ask him what was going on. However, his heavy eyes closed, and soon he was back in the land of dreams. He would have little memory of this dream in the morning. Though sometimes, as with dreams, things throughout the day can bring them back to mind.

Halvor the Wizard

Timmy tucked into his breakfast and looked forward to his second day exploring. Was all this a dream? His mum would say that he had a vivid imagination and could tell good stories, probably because he had grown up with narratives of people he had never met and places he had never been. He thought Origen seemed clear about who he was, a simple yet wise man's voice with a gentle fatherly tone. Timmy had begun to think of himself as a person, not just the son of his parents. But what next?

There was more wind today, so Timmy put on his thick jacket before he set out with Origen. His mother smiled curiously as she heard him say, "Good morning, Origen. What will we see today?"

Once they entered the wood, the wind blew stronger. It stirred up leaves into spirals and Timmy watched them intently. "It's as if the wind is drawing shapes in the air."

"*Yes,*" Origen replied. "*The wind can be gentle yet strong enough to blow down trees. See how these trees lean slightly to the left? That's because the prevailing winds blow from the opposite direction, causing the trees to grow that way.*"

They stopped in the shelter of a bush for a while and watched the leaves dancing in the wind. One group of leaves was swirling the opposite way round from the rest.

"*Very strange,*" Origen remarked. "*I have never seen that before.*"

They remained quiet as the leaves grew to almost six feet and formed into the figure of a man. Timmy wanted to run but was too scared, so instead, he held on tightly to Origen, his back pressed against a tree. He could make out the shape of what looked like a man in a broken pointed hat with a large staff in his right hand, and with his left hand, he reached out to them.

"*It's Halvor the wizard, defender of the Earth,*" Origen said. "*We are safe. He will not harm us. Listen carefully.*"

The wind had dropped though the leaves held their shape, and then a quiet dry voice spoke, "Be aware of the darkness." With that, the leaves collapsed to the ground.

Timmy was shaking and said he would rather go back to the cottage, but Origen encouraged him to stay, so they could try to make sense of what had happened. Timmy trusted Origen, so he reluctantly agreed. Also, he knew Jack was close by as he had heard him in the trees, though everything had gone quiet when Halvor spoke.

"*That's the first time I have seen Halvor, though I know he can appear in many forms,*" Origen said. "*His name means Flat rock or Defender of the earth. He dates to the origin of the standing stones though would have been known by a different name then.*" As he said this, the wind picked up a little and moved the leaves in a line ahead of them. "*I have heard stories about him, of course, but I have not known what to believe. Many people create stories when they are not sure of things,*" Origen paused, "*for example, look at that branch up there. It looks like a snake.*"

Timmy gave a little start. It did.

"*But it's not,*" Origen continued, "*it's just a branch.*"

Timmy frowned. "So, were those only leaves blowing in the wind, or did we see Halvor?"

"*I believe Halvor used the wind and the leaves to give you an important message.*"

Timmy looked down. "Halvor told me to beware of the darkness, which means be afraid. I am afraid."

"*What Halvor said was to be aware of the darkness.*" Origen corrected him. "*It is quite different. Notice the darkness – be aware and not afraid of it.*" Timmy was still hanging on to his fear of the dark, unable to see where he was, what was around him, or if something was coming to harm him.

Origen heard Timmy's thoughts. "*You have nothing to fear, though you do not believe. Like the branch, once you knew it was only a branch, the fear left you.*"

This was easy for Origen to say, Timmy thought. He had lived with these fears all his life, and he knew they were real.

Walking further on through the wood and following the trail of leaves, Origen continued, "*Life is all about what we think we see, hear, and feel, and this is what creates the beliefs in which we live. It's far easier to believe that the sun, the moon, and the stars travel across the sky when in fact, it's we who are moving. We believe we are the most important thing in the Universe and that everything moves around us. The secret is to become the least important. From there, we can see the truth.*"

Timmy thought Origen was on to something and started to look at things differently. He's a clever old stick, he thought.

The rest of the day was fresh, the wind dropped, and the sun got out for a while. Timmy even took off his coat as he walked by a different path along the outer edge of the wood – a part where the farm vehicles did not go, so the grass grew longer. They crossed through the wood and the village then headed towards the cottage.

An elderly man came towards Timmy, commented on his fine stick, and wanted to know where he'd got it. Timmy at once moved Origen out of the man's reach and told him it was his grandad's. The man wanted to know if he would sell it. Timmy said a loud, *No*, but the man persisted. So, feeling threatened, Timmy ran and didn't stop until he reached the cottage.

His mother had seen him running, and as he came through the door, she asked, "Who's chasing you?"

"Nobody, well yes, the leaves," Timmy said. "It's a game I'm playing." He didn't want to alarm his mother.

She smiled. "Tea will be ready in fifteen minutes, so it's a good job you ran. You might have been late."

A Murder Mystery

It was early evening, and Timmy sat with his mum and Grandma comfortably in the living room. The household was quiet, a change for Timmy after recent events. He was living in two worlds. On the one hand, he was just Timmy. On the other hand, he was on an amazing adventure of wizards, waterfalls, and a magic stick.

Never having had a television, Grandma kept in touch with the world around her through friends. She had an old valve radio for news from further afield and entertainment. The downside of this radio was its size, and the time it took to warm up the valves. Highly polished with crystal clear sound, it was more like a piece of furniture. It was Tuesday, and a murder mystery play was being transmitted.

Timmy's mum listened closely as she tried to work out who the murderer was. "You have to listen out for clues," she said. "They are written into the script all the way through, though some are lies. Either to cover the murderer's tracks or to stop other people's guilty secrets being uncovered."

"How do you know which are true and which are lies?" Timmy said.

"It's not easy. That's what makes it such a good story." His mum unwrapped a toffee and popped it in her mouth, carefully folding the wrapper. "All becomes clear at the end, when the detective reveals the chain of events and motive, then finally the killer's identity."

Listening attentively to the story, Timmy suspected everyone. The toffees also helped his concentration. "It's a shame we can't fast forward the programme, like a cassette recorder, then we would know who done it."

Grandma frowned. "Where would be the fun in that? We would not learn anything." She leaned towards the radio and gave a loud *Shush* not wanting to miss a word. Timmy curled up his feet in the chair, determined to be the first person to work out who the murderer was.

The story was centred around the murder of a wealthy old man, who had been found dead in his locked bedroom. The murder weapon was presumed to be poison, and the prime suspect was Andrew, the old man's nephew. He only visited when there was something to be gained. However, it was discovered that the victim's wife was in possession of the bedroom key. Though if poison was the murder weapon, then perhaps the gardener would have knowledge of poisonous plants. There were so many potential false leads to follow.

Timmy scribbled notes on his sketch pad and listed evidence found against the suspects to keep up with the detective, which helped keep his mind focused on the task. At home, he would normally be in front of the television in a state of semi-consciousness – a television can do that. Despite Grandma's shush, Timmy dared to speak once more. "I bet the author wrote this book backwards. Deciding who the murderer was, then putting all the evidence together, revealing the plot page by page. He would have to put piles of misleading facts in there too, keeping it a mystery until the end. It would not be much fun for us to work out who'd done it halfway through the book. I bet I could write a story like that."

There was another loud *Shush* from Grandma.

With the programme only having five-minutes left and a climax fast approaching, the detective called everyone into the kitchen.

"Is it the cook?" Mum said. This time there was a long *Shush*, and Grandma tapped the chair arm with her fingers.

As with good mystery stories, there was an unexpected twist at the end. It turned out the murderer was someone whose family lost their home and business after being cheated by the old man many years ago. None of them had been aware that the newly employed maid was the daughter of the cheated family.

"That's not fair," Timmy said. "How could we have known that?"

His mum smiled. "Sometimes when everything else is ruled out, what remains is the truth. The maid had the means to do the deed, the opportunity and the motive, and she covered her tracks very well, pointing the finger at Andrew."

Grandma had nodded off and only opened her eyes when Timmy's mum mentioned making a cup of tea.

It was only eight o'clock, so Timmy decided to go and bring down one or two of his grandad's sketch pads. With a mug of tea and his feet curled up again, he thumbed through the pages. Grandad's drawing style was like his, and he felt this was a little weird as he had never seen them before. He stopped halfway through the second book and came upon something different instead of trees, birds, or something locally familiar. This drawing was more like a collage than a picture and was accompanied by a short poem with a sombre feel. The prominent feature was a cross on a hill and a military helmet and rifle, which had been drawn roughly and smoothed over with the artist's finger. Timmy thought this must be a memorial to his grandad's fallen comrades.

The poem read:
> *Resting in eternity*
> *Hidden from view*
> *Just a stone's throw*
> *From where the acorns fall*
>
> *Nothing is lost forever*
> *All will be as it was*
> *Beside the falling water*
> *In the crevasse of a rock*
>
> *Valour is not in a medal*
> *Nor in the mind of man*
> *It comes in on the wind*
> *And then it is gone*

These words were written about sacrifice and of those whom we lost. Timmy could not imagine the horrors of war, the deep desperation of doing your duty for King and country. He wondered – what was the point of it all?

As he climbed into his bed that night and closed his eyes, Timmy felt the darkness return in the shape of the man who had wanted Origen. Was that what Halvor had warned him about, and would that man come back? Timmy knew how special this stick was and never wanted to lose it.

Abandoned House

Another fine morning and Timmy and Origen were again in the woods. He stood and looked at a tree he had not noticed before. "This must be one of the oldest trees in the wood. It's huge and has branches as thick as the other tree trunks."

Origen offered a little background information. *"The tree has become something for which it was not intended. Locally, it is known as the Name Tree. People have carved their names and initials into its bark for over a hundred years. If you look, you will find your grandad's there too."* Timmy felt sorry for the tree but was also excited to see if he could find grandad's mark. He read through the plain and ornate text, some were clear, but others, faded by age, were barely recognisable. And there it was, high up, *T.B.*

Origen spoke softly, *"It's strange how people feel the need to leave a mark, a statement of their existence. This is me... I am here. Then they use initials, so they won't be accused of defacing a tree. It's natural to declare recognition of self or one we love. Many couples here have left their mark on the Name Tree, marks that remain long after the people have gone."*

"Is it possible to live forever?"

"For everything, there is a beginning and an end, and for each end, there can be new beginnings. However, immortality is often sought after, but never achieved."

Timmy ran his fingers over the tree bark. "Even these names don't last forever," he said. "Our memories last as long as we do and if we share them, perhaps a little longer."

"*You are becoming a very wise young man, Timmy Flea,*" Origen said as they wandered on.

It was midway through Timmy's week. Each day his walk would take him to the same woodland path. And each day, he would see something different. Everywhere he looked, there were mysteries to be solved, questions to be asked, and clues to uncover.

Timmy stopped, turned around, and strained his eyes to see. Before him was an overgrown path. Origen, who knew what he was thinking, said, "*It's the old path to Hollywell house. It's not been lived in for many years and now has no roof.*"

Timmy pointed the stick and headed into the undergrowth, pushing aside the long grass and ferns.

Origen was alarmed. "*Be careful, Timmy, the clue is in the name. This house is built next to a deep well.*"

About a hundred yards in, Timmy saw the ruined walls of an old house covered in types of creeping greenery. He explored the kitchen and downstairs rooms, more intent on going inside than finding the well. Peeking up the chimney to see where Jack lived, but he was not at home and the ceiling, and the floor above had gone. It seemed strange to see the sky above him. Timmy imagined the sound of children playing, a mother making dinner and a fire glowing in the hearth.

Origen began to tell their story, "*A young family were the last to live here, almost a hundred years ago. The house belonged to Castle Farm just outside the village, and when the farmer's son found a wife, he gave him Hollywell house. The son and his wife turned the house into a home while continuing to work on his father's farm. Soon there were children, and the family outgrew this small house. Then the family got a chance to own a farm themselves. No one wanted to live in a house without electricity or running water, so the house remained empty."*

Timmy thought he would have liked to live there, but washing in chilly water seemed grim. "Which way to the well?" he asked.

"We need to look for its guardian because every holy well has a tree guarding it," Origen explained.

Timmy thought Origen said holy well.

"I did," Origen answered, *"wells are sacred, holy and special. Life cannot exist without water. The guardian tree is often an Elm, an Oak, Ash or a Blackthorn, though we are looking for an old holly tree in this case."* And there it was, no more than twenty steps away. *"Be careful, Timmy, the walls of the well may be broken and loose,"* Origen called out. Timmy was already staring up at this majestic holly tree. Part of it may have been the family's Christmas tree.

Timmy felt himself slip, knew he was about to fall, and let out a scream as he went down, but somehow managed to grab hold of a tree root. He came to a halt at the edge of the well, peering into the darkness. There was a splash as a stone hit the water a long way down. Heart beating fast, he lay there for a moment. "Hey", he shouted, and the echo called back, "Hey." Timmy was still holding onto the root, and with his other hand, he took hold of Origen's head. "Is this what you mean by a guardian?" he asked.

"I guess so", Origen replied, and they both laughed.

Timmy sat cross-legged beside the well and imagined people with a bucket and rope, drawing water for washing and cooking. He wanted to taste the water but had no means of getting it.

Origen suggested they continue their walk and try to find a freshwater spring. He told Timmy to stop and listen a little further along the old path.

There was a faint trickling sound, so Timmy followed this until he came to a small pool of clear water.

This was indeed coming out of the ground, forming ripples across the pool, then flowing over and down towards the river.

"Is it okay to drink?" Timmy said. "I don't have a cup."

Origen suggested he cupped his hands and scoop up the water. He did so, and though it had no flavour at all, Timmy felt he tasted the whole of creation, earth, berries, and sunlight in one sip. This was so refreshing, much better than any bottled or tap water, and Timmy took two more long drinks. He thought today's sketch would be the old house with the holly tree in the background. Things that were hidden were coming to light.

Hidden Treasure

Timmy, still with thoughts of fresh flowing water, yet without conscious thought, walked along the riverbank heading towards the waterfall. "In science, we learned that water falls from the clouds to the ground, flows to the sea, and then rises back to the clouds. Do you think this river is the same water that's been running for hundreds of years?" he said.

"*Well, you do ask some interesting questions,*" Origen said. "*First, I don't think the same way you think. Knowledge is already there for me to put into words. I don't have to think about it. This is the same river that has been here since the ice age. It has changed direction slightly over the years and has widened a little as the softer ground was washed away by heavy rainfall. It is the same river, though the water that makes it a river is never the same. Every time we dip our hands into the running water, we touch something unique. The same elements in the water have never been together, nor will they ever be again. In the same way, your experiences combine to create your unique self.*"

Timmy didn't expect that kind of answer. There was always much more from Origen. But happy to ponder on the word unique, he decided not to follow with more questions.

As the water hit the steadfast rocks with a pulsating roar, the rushing waterfall sounded like the wind. When he reached it, Timmy sat down and took out his sketch pad, knowing that each time he drew anything, he would see it differently. With the sketch almost complete, he pencilled in some shading to one of the larger rocks. This rock looked familiar. Of course, he had seen it often. However, he sensed he had seen this in a different context, though where, eluded his conscious thinking. Timmy closed his eyes and listened to the water. In no time, he saw the sketch done by his grandad, the one with the cross and a military helmet. He opened his eyes and spotted the large rock in the waterfall. It was indeed the shape of that helmet.

Our imaginations race in numerous directions when confronted by curious incidents. The more he looked at the rock, the more he could see his grandad's sketch, which had to be explored further. Soon Timmy was scrambling over the large rock. Reaching the top with water flowing around him, he could see the riverbank from a different position. Beside the path he had often walked, was a large oak tree. Grandad's poem had spoken of a place where acorns fell. To his left was a crevasse in the rock, high enough to be out of reach of the flowing water. This experience was becoming more curious by the minute. He could not resist the urge to roll up his sleeve and thrust his arm into the crevasse. As he brought out leaves, the wind seemed to increase and carried them away. There were also twigs and other rubbish trapped down there over the years. His imagination ran ahead of him, and as if his fingers were stretching beyond their length, he explored the inside of the crevasse. Timmy repositioned his body to gain more depth. Then, his index finger touched something cold, metal, and sharp. This investigation had to be pursued until the object was brought to light. He needed to find two thin, long sticks to use as tweezers. Following his inner picture of the crevasse, Timmy fished around with the twigs he'd found, then something shifted deep inside, and excitement rose again. Time to go back in with his fingers, and they seized the item in a scissor action. He withdrew slowly, holding his breath, not wanting to drop it.

His heart could barely hold his excitement, and with the weather-worn medal resting in the palm of his hand, Timmy pondered on the poem's words. Did his grandad expect it to be found or prefer it to be buried forever? Should it be returned to where he found it or taken back to Grandma? He turned to Origen for advice.

The stick simply said, "*It's up to you.*"

How his grandad felt about the medal and how Timmy felt was different, and he decided to take it back to the cottage, clean it, and then put it with the sketch among grandad's collection of books.

Following the cleaning later that day, Grandma was amazed to hear Timmy's story and to hold the medal after so many years.

"You followed the clues and solved the mystery, young man. Well done. This will be yours one day. I was proud of your grandad and so relieved he came home when many of his friends didn't."

To say Timmy was pleased with himself would be an understatement. This was the first thing he had begun and completed on his own without being asked. Finding the medal was also special as it pleased his grandma.

The evening continued with a game of scrabble, which Timmy regarded more like spelling homework than a game. Grandma's health was improving with company and loving care. She also won the game. His final task was to place the medal with Grandad's belongings. He found a scrap of blue material, wrapped it carefully and laid it in a box.

All was well, and surely all would continue to be well. Timmy smiled contentedly, realising that there are important things to achieve in this world, even for young boys. It was only halfway through the week, and Timmy's secrets were multiplying ten-fold, recording everything in his sketchbook.

The Waterfall

The Inner Circle

Lost in the River

The next morning, Timmy's mother reminded him of the dangers in the wood with the rough, slippery paths, hidden rocks, and tree roots. You might have thought he was setting out on a dangerous expedition. He knew this was just his mum's way of caring, so he didn't listen. Setting out from the garden gate, he felt good about the day and looked forward to his conversations with Origen, who had become a close friend. They could hear Jack ahead of them on the edge of the wood, competing with other bird songs, though his was more of a harsh shout.

Timmy and Origen had become inseparable. Walking and talking together, they passed close to the river's edge, and then it happened. Timmy had only let go for one second, and the strap was not around his wrist. The stick fell, and Timmy screamed at the top of his voice. He ceased screaming when he saw the stick bounce into the river and head downstream. Timmy ran. He was off the path and trying to keep the stick in view. The fear of losing Origen would be too much to bear.

The stick stayed silent as it was thrown from side to side by the rushing water. Large rocks spun it around, yet on it went. Scratched by thorns and other stinging things, Timmy gasped for air as he ran fast, but the water turned the stick around and sent it into the bank – the opposite bank. Origen was stuck among tree roots, and Timmy couldn't get across. The only way was for him to return to the bridge and run along the other side to where it was resting. Timmy's heart pounded. He didn't want to let Origen out of sight, but there was no other way. What if the stick was gone when he got there, washed away by the water?

Once over the bridge, Timmy kept close to the river until he reached where he thought the stick would be. He noticed that Jack was sitting in a tree opposite as if keeping an eye on Origen. He flew off just as Timmy arrived on the scene. Due to the bank overhang, Timmy could not see the stick, so he got down on his tummy and leaned over. There was Origen, just out of reach, held fast by both the roots and the water. What could he do? He thought long and hard, pulled himself up quickly, and searched for a long stick. Some were too short, and some were not strong enough, but eventually, Timmy took hold of one that was exactly right and snapped off a small shoot at the end, leaving it like a hook. Before long, he was back on his tummy, trying to aim the hook through the leather strap without pushing the walking stick further into the river.

It was a delicate operation, but he brought the stick back to dry land after several attempts and hardly daring to breathe. Then, shaking, eyes watering, he sat back against an old tree and, holding the head of Origen tightly, he said, "I thought I had lost you."

Then Origen said a strange thing, "*Nothing is ever lost in this world.*"

Timmy was so pleased to have the walking stick in his hand that he hadn't noticed how wet, muddy, and scratched he was. Touching the stick, his fingers ran across the words *Hold on to what you have*.

Origen said, "*These words have nothing to do with physical things. They speak of holding on to who you are, your purpose, strength, generosity, and laughter.*"

Timmy smiled and decided it was time to go back to the cottage. Perhaps later, he would do some drawing. Crossing the bridge, he decided to take the easier route through the village.

Very few people were there that afternoon, so it was

The Inner Circle

not difficult to spot the elderly man sitting outside the café. Timmy recognised him as the man who had wanted his stick. He looked straight ahead and kept walking on the opposite side of the road away from the man.

"Timothy Walker," the man shouted.

Timmy froze. How did this man know his name? Origen remained silent throughout.

"My name is Crozier. I knew your grandad. Come on over."

Timmy hesitated and then crossed the road, feeling safer now that he had seen two other people inside the café.

"You look a bit of a state. What adventures have you been up to? Grab a seat. Can I get you a glass of pop?" The man rose to his feet, holding the back of his chair for support. This was not a man who could catch a young boy running, Timmy thought.

He was back with a glass of fizzy lemonade in a short while. Timmy had placed the stick down between himself and the chair. "Malcolm, pleased to meet you," the man said. "Sorry if I scared you last time."

Timmy sipped his lemonade and waited.

"Your grandad and I were great pals. We grew up together and went to school here in the village. I moved away but returned just before Ted died. I remember we were having a beer at the Star Inn one night and got talking about his stick. He told me it was special, even magical. But he wouldn't say anymore." There was an uneasy silence. "Tell me, Timothy Walker, how special is this stick?"

Timmy looked down into his glass and thought carefully before he spoke, "It's very special to me. It belonged to my grandad, whom I never met." He looked straight at Malcolm. "It's not for sale... What else can you tell me about my grandad?" Though

Timmy didn't realise it, he safely diverted the conversation away from Origen.

A story unfolded of Ted and Malcolm, who set out to the woods one day and built a den. Malcolm's eyes twinkled as he talked about Ted being the designer and supervisor of the project. Malcolm was the builder, the stronger of the two and content to do the arduous work. Ted's diligence was needed for the knots, holding the frame securely in place. "That would be the summer of 1930, and we were sixteen. We did have some fun, and the old den lasted well into the winter," Malcolm concluded.

Malcolm looked at Timmy's almost empty glass and asked if he wanted another, but Timmy politely declined and Malcolm continued, "We never thought there would be a second world war. Ted, the clever one, joined the Royal Engineers. He had a fascination for building bridges and blowing them up. I left to join the Royal Navy. That's when we lost touch because, after the War, I settled down in the south."

Malcolm finished his mug of tea and wiped his lips with his forefinger. "You can't beat a fresh scone and tea." He was preparing to leave, and Timmy was pleased. "So, you haven't noticed anything strange about your grandad's stick, then?"

Timmy shook his head, not wanting to get into that conversation.

"That's strange. I was sure Ted was holding back a secret. I would always know when he was scheming. Still, it's clearly in safe hands. Look after it well, young lad."

"Oh, I will, and thank you for the lemonade." They went their separate ways under better circumstances than their first encounter.

When he arrived at the cottage, apart from, "What kind of mess are you in?" his mum greeted him with what she thought was good news. "Your Aunty Anne and cousin Rebecca are visiting tomorrow."

Timmy frowned. That could only mean trouble.

Playing Cards

It was a bi-weekly event of playing cards at Grandma's cottage, which had been going on for years. Timmy's mum had prepared a simple supper, and Grandma, who had slept all afternoon, was bright and talkative as Uncle Bill and Mrs Baker arrived. Timmy declined their offer to play, but his mum was happy to join in. The four sat around a small card table while Timmy sat in an armchair, his arm hanging over the side of the chair and his thumb feeling the shape of Origen's head. Timmy formed the words in his mind, *"This is going to be a boring evening."*

Origen responded, *"That depends on you, young man. The universe is full of choices, including how we choose to feel. Choose to feel different, and things will be different."*

Timmy gave no response. It didn't make any sense. If boring things were happening out there, then we could expect to feel bored. In his mind, there was nothing he could do to change the situation.

His mum turned to him and suggested he take out his sketch pad and draw the card players.

"No, it's okay. I'm fine here, just thinking." Instead, he decided to amuse himself with a bit of storytelling. He imagined the scene of a sweltering evening in South America. Four wealthy people sat down to play cards. The stakes were high, as each player was out to win. Servants brought in drinks and a selection of bocaditos. The room was large, with ornate furniture and beautiful pictures hanging on the wall. The tall windows were open, and a gentle breeze wafted through the light curtain material.

The Inner Circle

Back in Grandma's cottage, the grown-up's conversation had quickly moved to stories of their early years. His mum was soon left behind as the other three were the same age. The talk was about family connections and schooldays, who belonged to whom and who didn't fit in. Timmy felt South America was far more interesting and continued to look around that impressive house. He was unaware of when he fell asleep, and his imaginings became strange dreams.

The people arriving at the grand house had become playing cards and came in order of colour and suit. The patterns on their backs varied, depending on the pack they belonged to. A Jack of Diamonds stood at the entrance and announced the arrival of each guest. *"Welcome to the two, three and four of Hearts."* There was a small cheer from the other Hearts in the room. Every card had its suit and number, and each knew its place in the pack. The Jack of Diamonds took a step back and said quietly, *"The Joker has arrived, my Lord."* A hush fell over the room, and many turned their backs, muttering to one another. No one would ever know what the Joker might do next. He was a wild card and could become any card he wanted. The Joker was decorated with Hearts, Spades, Diamonds, and Clubs. The King of Spades and his Ace boldly stepped forward. *"Now look here, Joker, you were not invited and should leave now,"* the King said.

"I am as much part of the pack as any other card, and I don't need an invite. I am the Joker."

The King of Spades gathered other Kings around him, and a lengthy debate began. *"We have order and numerical sequence,"* the King of Diamonds began. Clubs and Spades were sure that the pack would fall if he, the Joker, was let in. The Queen of Hearts wanted to show her caring side but was ignored.

"What do you think, Timmy? What do you think?"

"I think you should let the Joker in," Timmy said.

Uncle Bill laughed so much that he dropped his cards. Timmy realised he had been dreaming.

"Here you go, Timmy," Uncle Bill passed the Joker to him. "Take a closer look at this one. He looks a bit wild, don't you think?"

"I think it's sad, he is the most important card in the pack because he holds all the suits, but the others won't accept him," Timmy said. "Just because he is only one card – they are all bullies."

Timmy's mum went to the kitchen to put the cups and plates in the sink, while Mrs Baker and Uncle Bill went to collect their coats. Grandma looked across at Timmy. "It's kind of you to care for those who are ignored. That's nice to see."

After the guests had left, his mum helped Grandma up to bed, and Timmy began to fold down the camp bed. Covers and pillows all set, he went off to the bathroom to get into his pyjamas. Origen stayed with him as he snuggled down under the sheets. "Night, God bless," called his mum, and Timmy replied.

The silent conversation continued. *"Origen, how often is a Joker used in card games?"*

"Not very often, though there are games where the Joker is used."

"I guess people don't like things they are not sure of," Timmy said.

"That's right, we all prefer things to stay as they are, remain in order, or comply with the rules, which may or may not be right."

"I think he is a little like the wind. We don't always know which way it will blow or how strongly. Dad says weather forecasts are often wrong."

Over the last few days, so much had been happening that Timmy hadn't given his dad much thought. He felt awkward about that and began to think of home and wondered how things had been for his dad on his own. There were only two more days to go, and then back to school on Monday. Would he find life at home boring now, compared to here? Then again, the thought of Cousin Rebecca visiting tomorrow made him shiver.

Thunder and lightning

Cousin Rebecca was three years younger than Timmy, though you could imagine she was three years older. There was something about how she spoke – as if she knew everything. She was an only child and spoilt rotten. Everything she saw she wanted, and everything she wanted, she got. Timmy was fearful she would want what he now regarded as his walking stick, so he planned to set off early that morning before their visitors arrived.

This plan did not work, for as Timmy was gathering his things, there was a knock at the door. In ran Rebecca, followed by her mum. "Timmy Flea," Rebecca shouted. Timmy knew she was making fun of him. Rebecca never did anything nice unless she wanted something.

"Oh, are you going on a hike, Timmy?" Aunty Anne asked. "Rebecca can come with you."

Timmy looked at his mum for support, but her face said it all, and he could see it wasn't going to happen.

Aunty Anne fastened Rebecca's coat and tucked in her scarf. "Now, be careful out there and don't get in a mess. Listen to your elder cousin."

The reply of, "Yes, mum," was not convincing.

The young pair reached the garden gate. "I'm a fast walker," Timmy said. "You'll have to keep up."

Rebecca was not put off. "I'll need that walking stick then if I'm to walk fast."

"No, Grandma said I must look after this," Timmy replied quickly. Rebecca remained silent, which was unusual for her, but he knew she would not give in. His mum had suggested they should walk as far as the waterfall. This was quite far enough for Timmy with his unwanted company. Her silence was unbearable, as he knew she would be dreaming up something horrid.

Timmy saw the storm clouds gathering over the distant hills. If the wind changed, there could be rain. He already felt this would be a gloomy day with his little cousin tagging along so he tried pleasant conversation. "How's school? You must be in year seven now?"

"Yes," came her sharp reply. Timmy wondered how she had become so nasty. Her mum was genuinely lovely, though he didn't remember her dad as he had left the family just after Rebecca was born. He still felt the way she was, was her fault, and it was her job to fix it. Then he heard the voice of Origen, gently reminding him about judging others without knowing the whole story.

"I know," he said out loud.

Rebecca looked at him through narrowed eyes. "What?"

Timmy realised what had happened. "What, I mean no, err nothing."

She frowned. "You are funny, Timmy Flea."

They had made it to a narrow, uneven path and walked in single file. Timmy heard a scream and turned to find Rebecca on the ground.

"I've twisted my ankle," she said, "I'll need that stick now."

There, it had happened. Did she fake the fall? He didn't see it, though there were large stones, and a slip could easily have occurred. He helped her up, removed the strap from his wrist and handed her the walking stick. His thoughts were, would Origen speak to her, what would be her reaction, and could Origen's words change her?

Rebecca smirked and took hold of the stick. "Thank you," she muttered and marched ahead of him.

Timmy sighed as he followed close behind. "I think we should stop by the river," he called out, "so you can bathe your ankle in the cold water. It will help,"

"I'm fine," Rebecca said. "Is that the waterfall I can hear?"

Sure enough, just round the bend was the beautiful waterfall – the same waterfall but different water and a different experience. "Come on, let's sit on these stones," he suggested. "I'm going to soak my feet in the cool water. You can do what you want."

Before long, they were sitting side by side with their feet dangling in the water and Origen on the ground between them. They just listened to the sounds of the water without speaking.

After a brief time, there was a rumbling in the sky, which seemed to come from the ground, rise then bounce off the clouds as if they were bumping into one another. There was sure to be lightning too.

Rebecca grabbed Timmy's arm. "I don't like it," she said. It turned out Rebecca was more scared of the thunder than Timmy was, but he was not going to tell her that. He quietly put his hand on Origen and thought the word, *"Help!"*

As Origen began to speak with him, Timmy repeated his words out loud.

"Well, Rebecca, water droplets and ice crystals in the clouds rub together and create static electricity. The electricity builds up, and a lightning flash travels extremely fast from the clouds to the ground. Then there's a second flash returning to the clouds. The heat from the flash expands the air very quickly, and we hear the bang. There is often much rumbling too, as the air cools down." He let out a long breath.

Rebecca stared at him wide-eyed. "Oh, I see. It's not that scary now."

"That's right. Things are not so scary when we

understand what's happening."

"I'm scared of the dark, too," she said.

They decided to head back to the cottage, there was no rain, but it could still come. Rebecca did not pick up the stick, so Timmy did. It was like an unspoken way of saying thanks for making me feel better. Rebecca spoke about her school friends and homework projects. He saw a different side to her and hoped it would continue to be that way.

Aunty Anne and Rebecca left straight after tea. Having the visitors had cheered Grandma up, and she came downstairs and sat with them for an hour or so, reminiscing about days when Mum and Anne were young girls. His mum mentioned Malcolm Crozier.

Grandma's nose twitched, and she looked at me. "I remember Crozier, your grandad regarded him as a close friend, but I have always had my doubts about him. Ted was always accepting of others, never suspecting ulterior motives." This was out of character for Grandma, as she usually preferred to say nothing about someone rather than say something bad.

So much was happening, and time was going so quickly this week. Soon the cottage quietened down, and everyone was asleep. And this night, Origen lay on the floor next to Timmy.

The Universe

Though fast asleep, Timmy was aware of a noise in what he thought was the chimney. He woke with a start and sat upright on the camp bed. A small light shone through from the kitchen. Understanding Timmy's fear of the dark, his mum always left a light on somewhere. He took hold of Origen, "Are you asleep," he asked. "What was that noise?"

"I don't sleep," Origen replied, *"I don't need to. I think you will find it was just wind coming down the chimney, the universe entering the room."*

"There you go, saying strange things again. The universe consists of stars and galaxies, and they can't come down the chimney," he said out loud. Timmy knew a thing or two about planets and stars, as he and his dad often watched them from their back garden.

"The universe is all around us," Origen went on, *"not just beyond our planet. I can show you."*

Timmy got into his snug bed and said quietly, "No, thank you, I would rather stay here where it's warm and safe." He pulled the blanket under his chin, the stick held firmly in his hand inside the covers.

"Oh, it's quite safe," Origen continued, *"it may help if you close your eyes."*

Timmy felt he had no choice, and the journey was about to start, so he shut his eyes tightly and waited. There was no sudden revelation of light, just darkness. Timmy shuddered, but he trusted Origen's voice. There was absolute silence, no kitchen clock ticking, and no buzzing fridge. This was a peculiar feeling, leaving Timmy quite uncomfortable. Slowly, tiny specks of light appeared, and his instinct was to open his eyes. As

The Inner Circle

he did so, he could see no more than with his eyes shut. There was no room, no light coming in from the kitchen. He was somewhere else entirely.

Although afraid of the dark, he had no time to feel that fear. All his energy was focused on finding out where he was and what was happening. Slowly, as though someone was turning up the brightness, blues, greens, crimson, and striking gold appeared, swirls of bright clouds and dark shapes, everything frozen in time. "*Where on earth am I?*" the words stayed inside his head.

Then he heard Origen's voice, "*We are at the centre of the universe. You are seeing the pillars of creation. If you were looking from home, it would be within the Eagle nebula close to the constellation Serpens, but we are six thousand light-years from home.*"

Origen's answer left Timmy wondering. "*Yes, everything looks quite still. Yet everything is moving together extremely fast, just like when you're on the train, which may be doing sixty miles an hour, but you are sitting still and everyone else with you.*" Looking around him, Timmy could see millions of stars in every direction. One thing he didn't understand was why he couldn't see himself, not his body, arms, or legs. Yet he was there.

Origen continued, "*Dust clouds are rock particles, and rocks record history over millions of years. Dust comes from supernova explosions of stars which throw out a mixture of elements that come together to create the next generation of stars. This is cosmic dust, the stuff of which stars, planets and people are made.*"

"So, I am made of stardust?" Timmy gasped, and his eyes widened as he tried to take it in.

"*Oh yes, and so much more,*" Origen replied. "*Cosmic dust enters the earth's atmosphere and can easily come down our chimney. Think about how you can see dust in the room when bright sunlight shines through the window."*

Timmy was in awe of this vision but knew that he was dreaming. How else could this happen? He now wanted to wake up in his small bed, to see familiar light and hear the kitchen clock again. He felt the shape of a rock in his left hand. There had been masses of them all around him, suspended in space. The light faded the same way it began, and the sounds of the cottage returned. He was aware of the bedclothes around him, the stick, and a rock in his left hand. Exhausted, he fell asleep.

Morning came, and the rock fell beside him as Timmy rubbed his eyes. The dream came flooding back and he took hold of the stick. "Where did this rock come from?" he whispered. "It all seems like a dream."

"Every rock, tree, plant or person is unique, created from millions of particles. Like the stars and that rock, you are unique and special." Origen was speaking into the core of Timmy's being, a place of emotions, imagination, and reasoning. Now was the time to evaluate his position in the universe. Origen's words were spoken in a way that built foundations for strength and purpose. Timmy rolled the small rock in his hand and felt the crevasses and the smooth faces with his thumb. Origen was right. There can never be two things the same.

The morning's routine began with folding the camp bed and getting washed and dressed. At the same time, Timmy was looking out for stardust. There was little in the way of morning sunshine, though the darker parts of the room provided a background for the window light. Here he could see the dust particles suspended in the air, and when he blew on them, they swirled around in clouds like those in space.

Brushing his teeth, Timmy wondered how big is the

universe. How can we get our heads around infinity? Everything in the world, as we see it, has a beginning, middle, and end. We would have to join the beginning to the end to have infinity. So, endings are new beginnings? This was all a bit too much so early in the morning. His brain felt like it would explode. Perhaps we were not meant to think about such things.

The Inner Circle

A Dark Secret

Setting out on today's walk took them through the wood and towards fields facing Southwest. The weather was pleasant and sunny though there was a cool breeze. Timmy was surprised by how quickly time seemed to pass each day, yet how much slower the evenings were. Time, he thought, should be constant, something to rely on. Surely it was governed by the universe, marked by the separation of night and day, light and darkness. The seasons and cycles of life, all things keeping in time like one enormous clock, that the Master Magician wound up at the beginning of time. But what if time were to stop?

Timmy's thoughts were interrupted by Origen. *"It would be wrong to tell someone they think too much because thinking is an important part of who we are. However, we must keep things in the context of the part we play in this enormous clock and concern ourselves only with things that are important to us, things we can change."*

Timmy carried on with his silent narrative. *"My brain does hurt when I try to imagine the world without time. I wouldn't know when to go and catch a train. The driver would not know how fast or slow to go, so he arrived on time. But if there was no time, then that wouldn't matter."* As Timmy wrestled with these thoughts, his face pulled various strange shapes.

"Time, as we measure it today," Origen said, "has not been around long, only since the fifteen hundreds. However, to give order to our life in relation to each other, humanity has been playing with time, splitting it up into chunks since at least fifteen hundred BC. If you

The Inner Circle

said to your friend, 'I will meet you at the park at five o'clock,' they would know where and when to meet you. All time is calculated by the movement of the earth around the sun, which gives us the seasons. Daylight hours get longer then shorter, and all of this must be considered. Not to mention time zones in different places."

Timmy looked at his wristwatch. "My dad bought it for me, and it keeps good time."

"And you will set it against the clock at home, which your dad will check against the transmitted radio clock. We are all synchronised in time with each other. If we didn't measure and share time, our lives would be chaotic. However, if the solar system stopped spinning, then I have no idea what might happen and not knowing what's going to happen is often our greatest fear."

"Are there any secrets in the wood?" Timmy asked.

"If there were, I would not be the one to ask." As Timmy shuffled his feet and became more curious, Origen added, "Stories are told from long ago when there were trees as far as the eye can see, and within this small wood, they are still told today."

Timmy listened carefully and was keen to know more.

"There's a strange hill beyond the wood that resembles the shape of a dragon," Origen went on. "The dragon's name was Rune, a Norse word meaning 'secret.' Legend has it that Rune guards a stash of treasure that was stolen and hidden inside the hill."

Timmy's eyes widened, and his mouth dropped open. "Gold?"

"Many people thought so," Origen said, "and men went down to explore when a cave was discovered. The tunnels were said to be labyrinthine, where men went around in circles for days, and eventually, all searches for treasure were given up. This dark cave became known as the *Uggr* cave, another Norse word that means 'something to be feared.' People were reluctant to enter, fearful of becoming lost, and there were stories of strange beasts."

"But what is the truth?" Timmy persisted, who would love to see these things for himself.

There was a pause, and Timmy thought Origen was stuck for an answer. *"There are many things we will never know for sure, and stories are often only stories. Yet sometimes, hidden within them are words of truth. It is said that a young man in search of gold entered Uggr cave one day, and though he never found any gold, he was fearful that others would come and find it before him. It was said he went mad in there and eventually died. Again, these may be only stories to keep people out."*

They made their way to the southern edge of the wood. *"There's Rune hill,"* Origen said. *"Can you see the dragon?"*

"Yes, there's his head and back." Timmy took out his sketch pad and began to draw. The quick sketch was somewhat exaggerated, as his use of heavy shading made it look more like a scary dragon than a hill.

But no matter how Timmy persisted, Origen would not be pressed to give directions to the cave entrance. *"You are too young to think about going in there."* From this distance, Timmy was brave and imagined himself as a great explorer. But Origen said, *"It's so dark in there you would not be able to see your hand in front of you."* In Timmy's mind, he'd already been equipped with a torch and rope.

"Young men and their talk, it's the same through all generations. You will learn that bravery is not something you can prepare for. It comes with the moment."

Timmy was full of questions. "Was there really a dragon, fierce or friendly?"

There was a hint of laughter in Origen's voice. *"I don't know. There have always been strange beasts, real and mythical. And there still are today if you look for them. Many creatures do not want to be found, so we may walk right past them and never see them because they don't exist in our reality."*

Timmy pondered on this for a while and then asked, "My world is tiny if it only consists of things I know or am aware of. Your world is huge, and you can see beyond what is visible. I'm looking forward to growing up and seeing the world unfold. Perhaps I will see dragons?" He began to take his thoughts further. Origen was not a live stick, but he knew so many things that Timmy started to wonder if he existed outside of time, having magic that enabled him to communicate with the natural world, which would make sense. Once again, Timmy felt as if his head would explode. "Are you outside time, and can you see the future?"

"It is a mystery to me about where I am in relation to time. I cannot communicate future events, even though I know of them. I have moments in time and space when I can see, hear and feel all things – past, present and future, but I cannot speak of them."

Timmy didn't want this week to end, but he would be going home tomorrow evening and leaving all this behind him.

"You're not leaving if you take it with you."

"How can I take it with me?" Timmy replied. "Surely that's impossible?"

"Hold your memories of these events in your mind. Imagine you are here within the wood. Remember the sounds and even the smells. Then, at those moments, it will be as if you are right here, becoming relaxed and refreshed."

The Inner Circle

Rune Hill

Going Home

The next morning Timmy was awake early. He helped himself to breakfast and left a note for his mum, saying he had gone for a walk and would be back for lunch. The sun had not long risen, and the birds sang through the crisp morning air. He stopped at the garden gate, rested his chin on the head of the stick and listened. There seemed to be hundreds of blackbirds singing to each other. He closed his eyes and could hear each bird and where it was as it took its turn to sing. Whether the song was close by, further into the wood or beyond, it was truly a magical moment.

Perhaps because it was his last day, this morning was slightly different. Closing the gate, Timmy paused and turned to look the other way. Across the road from Grandma's, was Castle Farm, also a sign that read 'Public Footpath,' and that was all Timmy needed to set off in a new direction. The path was little used and difficult to see, but spotting a stile across the field, he headed that way. He climbed the stile and saw, beyond the large hedges, ruins of an old castle. "I should have guessed that from the farm's name," he said to himself. "Strange that no one had ever mentioned it." Low walls outlined what must have been more of a small fortress than a castle, but an impressive circular tower complete with battlements stood intact. There, nature had taken over, and ivy crept up around the stonework. Timmy was unsure if the path even led past the castle but couldn't resist the thought of exploring, and he only had this one day left.

Reaching the castle, he stood with his back to the

tower. From there, he could see all nine stones of the circle and, beyond them, in the distance, the dragon's head of Rune hill. Timmy did not need a compass bearing to see that these three landmarks created a perfectly straight line running due east to west, with Low Standing to the south and Grandma's cottage to the north of it. "Surely that must be significant?"

Timmy took in the view for a while, then began to walk back. As he approached the stile, Origen offered his opinion. *"Significant or coincidental, it will be whatever we decide to make of it."* Timmy pulled out his sketch pad and, from his standing position, quickly marked out the lie of the land. Rune hill had to be the oldest feature, followed by the stone circle. The castle must have been built much later, commanding an impressive view. The farm he could see was undoubtedly built from the original castle stone. Mr Crozier owned it, and Timmy didn't want to bump into him.

Timmy considered the events of the week and that we learn through experiencing life's cycle of interactions – both the good and the bad.

"You must be part of the universe to see it," Origen said. *"Then all is one, and when we are one with everything, we will see things very differently."* Timmy felt Origen was becoming unfathomable. *"When we discover who we are, we find strength in our weakness. Unity in our emptiness and all the hope we need for tomorrow. We are never alone. We are all bound together with nature."*

Before long, Timmy was back at the waterfall. The noise of the water became deeper and deeper as the white foam flowed over the rocks. A change in the sound made Timmy stop and stare. Then, as the volume of water grew, the impossible happened. Someone was coming out of it. *"It's Halvor,"* Origen said. *"We are safe."*

As before, the water took on the same shape as the leaves, outlining the figure of the wizard. Then, whole, and dry, Halvor stepped out onto the bank. His robes were shades of green and brown, and he held a tall wooden staff, the top of which, a crystal stone of pure white light flickered as he spoke.

"It's all right, boy. I'm not going to turn you into a frog." Timmy was speechless, though he gave a nervous laugh. "You should listen more carefully," Halvor continued. "Beware the Puppet Master. Never seen but ever present, pulling your strings, manipulating you. Whenever you do thoughtless, unkind things, just because they are easier to do, that is the Puppet Master's work. He doesn't want you to become strong and he needs to remain in control. You must cut these strings so that you can be free."

Timmy could see the sense in this. There'd often been times when things could have gone much better, but it had been much easier to follow that invisible guide.

"Your light is so clear," Timmy said.

"My light is pure because it's made up of all the colours of the rainbow, and in that unity lies my strength. Now the Puppet Master's colour is red."

"Red for danger?" Timmy asked.

"It could be. However, red is also the first colour of the rainbow, has the lowest visible frequency, and holds the least amount of energy. It's an attractive colour that lures us in and then traps us."

Timmy frowned. "But how can I cut those strings if I can't see them?"

"It's easier than you think. Take away the Puppet Master's power, and the strings will fall," Halvor said. "His power lies in only what you allow. Begin to choose the better way of kindness and consider all colours equal. Remember, he is only one colour and can never succeed alone. Anything is possible when your hands are not tied."

Timmy held out his hands in front of him and imagined the future.

Halvor smiled. "That's right, open your mind to that future." Then he spoke in a strange language, and Timmy saw many future moments that filled him with joy and satisfaction. Even pain had meaning.

"Woah," Timmy said, "I am not on my own. I'm part of the universe."

"You're right," Halvor said. Then he walked away and vanished into thin air.

This had the hallmarks of a commissioning speech. These were words to remember always.

"I have very little left to add," Origen said, *"except, hold on to what you have. You have all you need."*

The afternoon dragged, bags were packed and ready to go, but Mrs Baker's arrival and their leaving time would be decided by the clock. Timmy busied himself with a box of Grandad's books and sketches to fill in the time. Outside he could hear Jack's chattering in the distance.

His mum came into the room and looked around. "I hope you are going to put all that away, Timmy."

"Yes, Mum. I've had a wonderful week. And I feel I have grown up so much. I have decided I would like to be called Tim. Timmy is a little boy's name, and that's not me anymore."

His mum smiled. "Well, young man, it will take me a little while to get used to it, but if that's what you want. Now, Mrs Baker will be here soon. Let's go catch that train."

Grandma's health had significantly improved. She now needed to take things slowly, and they'd be back to see her soon, hopefully with Dad too. Tim took his memories and thoughts with him, though he left the stick to hang silently on a hook behind the door.

During the train journey, Tim took out his sketch pad and thumbed through the pages, reliving the story of the week's events. He could never speak about the things that had happened. Origen, Jack, the Wizard in the wind and the water, a journey to the centre of the universe, Dragon hill, the stone circle and today, a castle. What if the standing stones really were crumbling? What would happen then? Was it all just a story, or was everything coming to an end?

The endless rhythm of the train wheels on the track lulled Tim to sleep, and he didn't wake up until they reached their destination. His dad was there to meet them.

"Hi love, hi, Timmy. Good to have you back." Tim's parents hugged.

Tim held out his hand. "It's Tim from now on, Dad. Just Tim."

"You've grown up, my boy." Dad shook Tim's hand and corrected himself. "Young man. You'll not want a cuddle anymore, then?" Tim pressed into his dad, put his arm around him and gave him a tight squeeze.

Peter

Five years passed, such a long time for a young lad. There had been more than a few trips to Grandma's cottage, though non like the one back in 1980. Conversations with Origen took on a more grown-up nature, and topics like dragons and wizards had faded.

Tim was not academic. He was a daydreamer. The teachers said that reasonable final exam results couldn't be expected. Yet on leaving school, he went on to college to study Maths and Science, though his dad would have preferred him to learn a trade that could secure his future. Six months into Timmy's course, an opportunity arose to work at a local warehouse, where he would earn money and go out with his friends. The warehouse was only a short cycle away, and with manual labour, he soon began to fill out.

Timmy had truly become Tim, which suited his new image and lifestyle. Workmates accepted the young recruit and helped him settle in. He had a decent work ethic, keeping stock tidy and in its proper places. Things were going well for Tim.

Early one Saturday evening, he was alone in the front room, sitting upright in the armchair, staring at the wall with a newspaper on his lap. He had heard the news earlier that morning and now saw it in black and white.

Peter and he had stayed close friends, even after leaving school. They'd often go downtown together on a Friday night to the cinema or bowling. Occasionally they would meet with other friends and recount their exploits.

The night before, Peter had been downtown alone because Tim was working late and had decided not to follow on. It was believed that Peter had stumbled into a group of lads taunting another, on his own. He had tried to stop them, and in the struggle, one lad pulled a knife, and Peter was left bleeding on the pavement. He died shortly after. Devastated, angry and numb, Tim felt like his entire world had collapsed.

The door opened – it was his mum. "Do you fancy a cup of tea?"

Tim said he would, and as his mum left, his dad came in and sat in the opposite chair.

"How are you feeling now, son?"

This seemed such a crazy question that Tim felt like swearing at him, but this was his dad, after all.

"I've been thinking," Tim began, "perhaps a few days away will help, just until the funeral. I could go and stay with Grandma."

When Mum caught up with the conversation, it was all agreed. Tim would leave on the 9.30 train the following day, taking his bike with him so he could cycle from the station to the cottage. Sleep was going to be difficult that night, so he put clothes and essentials into a backpack to keep himself busy. He'd need to travel light for the cycling leg of the journey. He paused to browse his old sketchpad before burying it in the bag between two shirts.

The train journey seemed much longer than Tim remembered, and he was surprised when the station clock confirmed that the train had arrived on time. He retrieved his bike and set off for the cottage, wanting to get there as quickly as possible to let Grandma know he had arrived safely. Cycling past the stone circle was heartening and the place he wanted to be with Origen.

Grandma came out to greet him. She looked well.

"Hi, Grandma, I'll just put my bike in the shed."

She smiled. "You must be hungry. I've put some lunch on the table. Come on in and wash your hands." She spoke to Tim's mum like this, too, as if she was still a little girl, but that was Grandma. "How was the journey, and how are you enjoying work?" she asked, avoiding any mention of Peter.

"I'm doing fine, and work is good... I need a little space, that's all."

"I know, I know," Grandma said, giving his shoulder a gentle squeeze. The two of them sat down to eat, saying little, but finally, Grandma broke the silence. "I've been sorting out that little room. Mrs Baker helped me get the camp bed ready for you. It's quite cosy. Just pop your things upstairs when you are ready, and I'll clear up down here."

Hearing the familiar sounds of doors and floorboards as he carried his bag up the back stairs, Tim felt he could rest peacefully here. Grandma and Mrs Baker had been busy, and he hoped it was not only on his account. The old walking stick was where he had left it, and he rested his hand gently on the head, "Hello, old friend, it's been a while. I have a lot to tell you, but it will wait until later."

"It's been no time at all since last we met," Origen replied softly, *"and for me, no time will pass until we speak again."* For Origen, it appeared that nothing in the world existed except the time they spent talking together, which reassured Tim and made him feel special.

All the boxes were still there, though now they had been labelled and stacked neatly to one side. The camp bed was under the skylight, and Tim thought of all the stars he might see. He also hoped Jack would not come knocking on the window. Sliding the bed slightly to one side, he sat on the edge and decided to browse through one of his grandad's sketch pads. In it were birds of all shapes and sizes, and Tim was pleased to see

The Inner Circle

a drawing of Jack like the one he had drawn.

As much as Tim wanted to go to the stone circle, he decided to spend the rest of the day with Grandma. They talked, played cards, drank tea, and retold stories. Tim was fiddling with the Joker card. "Are you going to let him in?" Grandma asked.

He remembered the time when he had the dream about playing cards. "Let him in to what?" Tim replied.

"He's a wild card, and once you let him in, everything changes."

Tim understood that his grandma was talking about something more profound than a game of cards.

Before long, it was her bedtime. "You can be the man of the house. You can lock up. See you in the morning. Sleep tight."

"Night, Grandma." The task of locking doors was simple, but with it came a sense of responsibility of being asked to do something that Grandma or his mum had always done.

Circle of Tears

Tim began breakfast by putting bacon under the grill. "I'll pop to the shop later and get some more supplies for us," he said, taking three or four mushrooms from the fridge.

Grandma laughed. "I guess you are growing up now, fending for yourself. There soon won't be much left for me to do." She brought out the bread and began to slice and butter as much as she thought they'd need.

"I love to hear your stories," Tim said, plating up the breakfast. "I am sure there are hundreds more you could tell."

"Oh, you've given me too much. I'll never eat all that," she said. "I don't need as much as I used to. Just a child's portion will do for me."

"I thought I would head out through the woods to the stone circle this morning."

"You're just like your grandad. He spent hours walking too. Of course, we didn't have a car in those days." She left a piece of bacon on her plate. "Pop that in a sandwich and take it with you, and there's a flask in the cupboard for tea. I guess you will be taking your grandad's walking stick too. He always said it was magical. I used to imagine him flying on it like a broomstick." They both laughed. When they had finished eating, Tim got ready for his walk.

The walk always began with the click of the latch on the garden gate. He would walk with Origen in his hand across the field to the wood, following close to the hedge. That way, Tim could spot more things. Once into the wood, he would follow the path past the bridge, and the waterfall, then cut across to the left and out into the field where the stone circle was perched on a hill. It was not the most direct route, but it was far more pleasant and would give him time to gather his thoughts.

There was a silence between Tim and Origen, but there were loads of sounds in the wood, and he knew Jack was always close by. When Tim reached the circle, he sat down against the Portal stone with Origen laid across his lap and his left hand resting on the carved head.

The stones seemed smaller than he remembered them, and sitting on top of the third stone to the right was Jack, head lowered and unusually quiet.

"It's not fair!" Tim shouted at the top of his voice. The sound echoed around the circle. "Why do these things happen, and why Peter? He did nothing wrong and didn't deserve that." Tim was desperate to blame someone. The lad with the knife was not his target. He was aiming much higher.

He looked down at Origen. "If there is so much magic in you, why can't you stop things like this from happening?"

There was a pause, and then Origen replied. *"I'm part of nature, not MASTER of it."*

"Then who is the Master Magician? Why won't he stop these people?"

"If the Creator holds onto what he creates, it can never fully become all it was created to be. To love is to let go, offering the freedom to choose and to grow, hopefully in the way we are intended to." Origen paused. *"Our purpose is to love. And when we do not love, we must forgive – ourselves and others. The path of peace is the hardest one to walk. Too often, it is easier to be angry in the heat of the moment."*

"But Peter died. Why couldn't he be saved? It's so

unfair. The lad who stabbed him is still alive."

"It's at times like this, that you must hold on to your love for your friend. Love is eternal."

Tim wiped his cheeks with his sleeve. Long deep sobs were held within the safety of the circle. Healing had started that would continue over the years.

Tim rested for a while with many thoughts surrounding him. Experiencing joyful memories of family, friends, and time spent alone in the circle. A sense of peace descended upon him, and he became aware of sounds coming from far and wide, yet so close he could touch them. He stood up. "I feel much better now. Shall we go?"

"Not yet", Origen replied. *"You need to remember this moment for future encounters. Do you trust me?"*

"I do trust you," Tim said.

"Put aside all your worries, let all external sounds disappear, and focus on the silence of the circle." Origen's words were calm and reassuring. *"Simply follow my instructions, and I will hold you."*

Tim recalled his journey to the Pillars of Creation. "Shall I close my eyes as I did before?"

"No, simply trust me," Origen said and then spoke some words in a language Tim had never heard before, then he said. *"Keep me firmly in your right hand and open your arms wide. Take a deep breath. Then rise as far as you can on tiptoe."*

As Tim followed these instructions, he experienced a strange sensation as his toes left the ground and he began rising above his full height. He continued to rise, two feet, five feet and more until he was on a level with the top of the Portal Stone.

"Lean slightly to your left, Tim." As he did so, he began to travel around the circle in a clockwise direction. It was a most exhilarating experience. As he drew level with the top of the Portal Stone again, Peter

appeared with no sign of harm or pain and a smile on his face. Then, reaching out and touching Tim's shoulder, he vanished. Origen lowered Tim down gently and gave him time to process what had happened.

They walked back through the village and approached the cottage in silence. Grandma greeted Tim with, "You have rosy cheeks. I think the wind has caught your face." Tim was not going to tell her about his flight around the standing stones and agreed it must be the wind.

Secret Cavern

The next day, as if something was drawing him there, Tim sought out the ruined castle, but when he spoke about this to Origen, no credible answer was given. It was difficult to see a path from the road, but Tim followed as he remembered it. Even the stile had been replaced by a larger fence and it looked like access was being discouraged. Nevertheless, knowing he was within his rights, Tim pressed on and found the castle as he saw it last time.

"What do you think you are doing?" a voice called out.

Tim spun around. "Sorry, but this *is* a public footpath."

"It's also my land, and I ask the questions."

Tim found the young man very rude. He was about the same age as Tim and looked like he might turn nasty. He decided to take the better way. "I'm Tim and I'm just out for a walk. Nice to meet you."

The young man's voice softened, "My name's Luke Crozier." He explained that his uncle had passed away, leaving him the old farm and the castle. "That's a nice stick", he added. "Could I see it?"

Tim had been afraid of Luke's uncle Malcolm, who'd wanted the stick for himself, so this gave him a feeling of déjà vu, but he was stronger now, more confident. "It's just an ordinary walking stick, but it's special to me as my grandad carved the head." He remembered his grandma saying Malcolm was not to be trusted, and now he wasn't sure about Luke.

"My uncle read many books about magic and

alchemy," Luke said, "and he'd studied the symbols on the standing stones. He told me that your grandad's stick had magical powers. There's certainly some strong magic around here, and I think you, me, and that stick could release that power. Don't you see? We were meant to meet here today."

Tim didn't know what to say. Part of him wanted to run away, but much of what Luke said made sense. What if the crumbling of the stones could be stopped? Origen remained silent, yet something was happening. The stick in Tim's hand was getting warmer, and he felt it tugging him towards the castle. This was new, and it made him uncomfortable. Origen obviously wanted him to move towards the tower, but why did he not speak?

Tim slowly stepped towards the tower, Luke followed, and as the two young men continued talking, Luke turned out to be truly knowledgeable about the symbols on the stones. Before either knew it, they were standing next to a pile of stones with a bush growing out of them.

"How did you know this was here?" Luke asked. "Your stick is magic, isn't it?"

Tim was back on the defensive. "No, I don't know what you mean. This is just a bush." Origen had returned to his normal temperature, though Tim's hands were sweaty by now, and his pulse was racing. However, he stayed in control.

Luke took a deep breath. "I will have to trust you, but you must promise to tell no one. I still believe we can work together. There are secrets down here that possibly only we can uncover the truth of." He parted the bush to reveal a small opening, going down under the ground. "Follow me, and you'll soon see what I am talking about. It's a tight squeeze but quite safe."

The tunnel was narrow, and until Luke shone his

torch, very dark. The two of them scrambled down for twenty feet or more, after which the tunnel levelled out and opened into a large circular cavern, thirty feet or so across.

Luke held out his hands. "Here we are. It's like a church, isn't it?" Luke's voice got louder, and he smiled. "Look at the symbols on the walls. Some are the same as the ones on the standing stones. By my reckoning, this cavern was here long before the castle was built and has been kept secret. My uncle discovered it by accident one day and studied the symbols until the day he died. He believed Alchemy could turn base metals into gold and unlock eternal life."

Tim remained cautious but felt drawn towards a large circle of eight gemstones, each the size of a man's hand. There was a hole where a ninth stone had been. He ran a finger all around the hole, and then, spreading out all his fingers, he placed his hand over the space.

"You've got it," Luke said and clapped his hands together. "We need to complete the circle by finding that missing stone. I think we can do it together. Isn't that exciting?"

"It's witchcraft," Tim said.

"No, it's alchemy. It's an ancient source of knowledge, and I mean to unlock its secrets."

"You are messing with things you don't understand, and I don't think I want any part of it. Your secret is safe with me, though." Tim thought the missing stone could be causing an imbalance and crumbling of the standing stones. Maybe, the legend was true. If this was left to continue, time itself would collapse. But suspecting that Luke was motivated by self-interest, Tim turned away and headed back to the tunnel. Luke tried to stop him by arguing, even offering a share of power with him.

The Inner Circle

Tim turned and held his ground. "You're right. My stick does have magical powers. It will tell me what to do. I'm leaving now, Luke, but I will come back, and when I do, I'll tell you how things will be."

Luke's face dropped, he had never been spoken to like that before, but he knew he could never complete the task without Tim and his magic stick. So, he followed him back up to the surface, and as Tim headed off towards Grandma's cottage, he shouted after Tim, "You will come back, won't you? This is important work."

"Yes, I promise." Tim wished he hadn't told Luke about Origen and worried about the consequences.

When they were only a field away from the castle, Origen spoke at last. *"You did well. I couldn't speak before because the magic there was too strong for mine. Remember Rune hill,"* Origen continued, *"and the story of the dragon and the stolen treasure?"*

Tim instinctively understood his words. The mystery was becoming much clearer now, and he knew what he must do, and quickly.

The Dark Cave

Tim set off on that straight line between the castle and Dragon hill, making for the stone circle. *"I know where you are going,"* Origen said. *"But have you thought this through, and do you know what you are taking on?"*

"In your words Origen... Yes and no. I am sure the missing stone is hidden inside the hill, and I must go into the cave to find it. It has to be brought back to its original place in the circle of nine gemstones, then that will bring everything back to normal, the stones will not collapse, and time will continue."

"What about Luke?"

"Luke will have to figure things out for himself. His motivation is selfish greed, so he cannot win this battle. I am stronger, and I have you."

Reaching the stone circle, Tim gathered his strength and his thoughts. The idea of going into the darkness and the unknown scared him. He began to doubt himself and wondered what skills or even weapons he might need. He popped five stones into his pocket and smiled to himself. What use would they be against a dragon?

Origen, attentive as ever to Tim's thoughts, spoke, *"When going into battle, you need armour. The belt around your waist symbolises the belt of Truth, your shield is a shield of Faith to deflect blows from the enemy, and your sword is a sword of the Spirit – the Word."* There was a pause before Origen continued. *"I cannot enter the cave with you. It is forbidden for me to assist you in this quest."* Tim's heart sank, though something inside pressed him forward.

"Let's go. Show me the cave entrance. I can do this." Leaving the circle, he did what he had often done before. Walking around the stones clockwise, he touched each one, reassuring the stones and himself that all would be well.

There were no paths to follow, just a straight line as if it were drawn across the fields for about two miles. When they arrived, Origen showed the area where there had been activity over the years. *"You must leave me here, Tim. The rest is up to you. Don't be afraid."*

The first entrance was wide, and it was easy to see how many people had come this far. The light faded as he went further in, and among some old equipment was a lantern still having oil. If only he had a match. Putting his hand into his pocket, he brought out the five stones. They were flint, and he managed to light the wick after several striking attempts. The flame was dim but just bright enough to light the way.

Twenty yards in, the temperature dropped significantly, and there was little air movement. To prevent himself from going around in circles, Tim marked letter Ts and a selection of arrow marks on the walls with one of his stones. Occasionally he heard sounds and knew he was not alone. It was difficult to know just how far he'd walked. The lantern flickered, then dimmed. As his eyes adjusted to the dark, he became aware of a presence, and it was coming towards him. The figure of a man loomed out of the shadows. A man so dark that the rest of the area appeared light in comparison. "I'm not afraid of you," Tim said in a firm voice. The figure came closer. "I am protected by the Belt of Truth and declare you are not real." Holding his forearm horizontally ahead of him, he added, "I carry the Shield of Faith and believe firmly in the truth of all that is good. You cannot harm me." Taking a fighting stance, he declared. "I hold the Sword of the Spirit – therefore, be gone in the name of the LIGHT."

He heard Origen's words, '*Hold on to what you have.*' Tim was not going to back down. All fear had left him – he was invincible. The total darkness of the figure began to disintegrate, and as it disappeared, the missing stone fell to the floor. Tim quickly knelt and picked it up, his heart beating fast. "It is almost done," he said, clasping the stone to his breast with both hands. "Now, to return the stone to its rightful place and convince Luke that all this had nothing to do with power."

With his eyes fully adjusted to the low light of the lantern, Tim followed his scratch marks back to the cave entrance and the full light of day. He sat beside Origen, head lowered, hands over his eyes, still shaking from the ordeal. Then putting his hand into his pocket, he brought out the missing stone. When he held it high, it glowed green in his hand, and he saw it was pure crystal. "I got it, Origen. I got it."

"*And what can you tell me about the darkness?*"

"I overcame the darkness. I don't think it will be around anymore. There is nothing for it to hold, no reason for it to be there." Tim had regained his composure and just wanted to complete the task. "We must get back to the cavern before the day is out. I don't want to risk anything stopping us now." Then, retracing his footsteps across the fields to the centre of the stone circle, he paused for a moment and gave a victory cry, "All will be well. I have the stone." The answering rumble from deep down under the ground shook him, but recovering quickly, he set off and ran the rest of the way to the castle.

The Inner Circle

The Castle

Setting things Right

Luke was sitting by the entrance, and the book he was reading fell to the ground as he jumped up. "Have you got it?" he shouted. "Do you have the stone?" He narrowed his eyes and studied Tim. "Give it to me quickly, for the sun will soon be setting."

"No," Tim said, "this is mine to finish. I will be the one to replace the stone. You can carry on with your incantation if you wish. I am trusting in the truth."

Luke smiled and stood aside, letting Tim in first. The descent was more of a falling slide as they rushed the last few feet. Once in the cavern, Tim headed towards the circle of stones, then hesitated for a moment as Luke recited words from one of his books.

Turning the stone ninety degrees, Tim placed it in the hole in the wall. It was a perfect fit. Nothing happened – what had he expected?

Luke continued to chant. Almost a minute went by, and then the young men were transfixed as a faint light began to radiate, first from the stone that had been missing, then in random sequence, each stone added to the display. By now, the light was flashing faster and faster.

"I'm leaving," Tim said, turning on his heels. Luke hesitated, then followed close behind. Climbing out of the cavern became a scramble as they struggled to get a grip on the narrow incline.

They ran from the ruined castle but stopped as a tremendous rumbling vibrated beneath their feet and ran up their legs. Luke grabbed Tim's arm and held on to it tightly. They watched as what was left of the tower fell in upon itself, burying the cavern forever.

Luke was the first to speak, "This must never be

spoken of or reopened ever again. I was wrong to think I could control all that power. We could have been killed."

They were both still shaking from the experience. "You can live your life differently now, Luke. Now you are free of that obsession," Tim said. "I think we shall both be different from this day on." Tim picked up Origen, and bid Luke goodbye.

"Bye, Tim and thanks," Luke said. "I think I have some clearing out to do now of books I no longer need." The change in him seemed genuine, though that would remain to be seen. "I will contact the local council and tell them the collapse was due to ancient earthworks."

Tim wanted to go back to the stone circle and inspect the stones to see if there had been any change. Whether he had prevented the collapse of time would never be known, but would the stones still be crumbling? That would be good enough for him.

The sun had dipped behind the hills and night was approaching, but this did not deter him, and soon, he was once more within the circle. The symbols on the standing stones had mysteriously vanished, but they did indeed seem to be crumbling less, and as they stood majestically against distant dark grey clouds, they appeared to shimmer.

Tim felt much more energised, as though he could, and should, achieve anything he set his mind to. This sense of self-confidence and freedom from fear was deep within him. Tim had become a warrior, and his future life would be quite different.

On reaching the cottage, he was greeted by his grandmother. "I thought you had got lost. Come on in. You must be starving. I have some stew in a pot."

Now that was just what Tim wanted to hear. Stew was one of his favourites. It also helped him step back into his other world, the one connected to the folk he loved. The whole cottage was filled with the aroma of home cooking, and Grandma had even made some fresh bread buns.

"All is well," Tim said. "And all manner of things will be well."

"Where did you hear that?" Grandma said.

"I am not sure, but it is right, isn't it? All things will be well. It's just at the time when things are crazy that we get scared and feel lost."

"Come on. Let's eat while it's hot. Later we can play cards, with or without the Joker." Grandma laughed.

The events of the last twenty-four hours had overshadowed all thoughts of his friend Peter, but Tim had, in the silence of eating, begun to process Peter's death.

"Peter's not really gone, you know. I can still feel him around me, and he is still very real in my memories and thoughts."

Grandma smiled. "Your grandad never left me, nor did I want him to. No wonder boxes of his rubbish are still up in that small room. There will be some sorting out to do when I have gone, I tell you."

"I promise I will look after things for you, Grandma, but not for a while yet, eh?"

"Now then, let's leave the plates until later. We'll get the cards out and put the radio on. There was a game I used to play years ago called Newmarket. It's about backing horses. We can play for matchsticks. I don't want you going home telling your mum I was teaching you to gamble."

The game went on until Tim suggested they play one last hand and then turn in to bed, and as much as he had enjoyed his stay, now the task was complete, he was ready for home. He had also time to consider some words he would say at Peter's funeral.

On the day of Peter's funeral, it seemed that the whole town had turned out to show their support for his family. The media tried to say that Peter was a hero, giving his life for another. Tim was confused by the term hero, as Peter would not have had time to consider the consequences. To him, it was a senseless waste of life, taken by one whose own consequences will be small in comparison.

Tim and his family visited Grandma often over the next six years, and Tim would once again walk with Origen, keeping him up to date with his life. His sketch pad was rarely seen, but his drawing skill would return in later years. He was still living at home with his parents, from which some mickey-taking was made by his mates.

Tim was content with life, and although he did have girlfriends, he seemed happy not to get too involved. Perhaps he had not yet met the right girl. His social life revolved around workmates, pub quiz nights and basketball, though his greatest love was the outdoors and hiking with a small group of friends, both evening walks and adventures that sometimes lasted all weekend.

Grandma

November 1991 and Grandma left this world to join her beloved Ted. There was no warning. A sudden heart attack took her. She had said she felt a bit strange when Uncle Bill had called in for a cup of tea. He called the ambulance and held her hand until they arrived, but Grandma had slipped away without a fuss. It was a sad time though, and as the family gathered, many stories were shared. Tim was asked to be one of the four pallbearers carrying her to her resting place beside her husband and he accepted this great honour.

Grandma's story was simple. She was born in 1917 and christened Elizabeth at All Saints, the church where she was also buried. She was May queen in 1935 and met Ted Bell that same year. Married in 1940, Elizabeth and Ted brought up two girls. Ted died in 1965, but today they are together for eternity. Of course, there is much more between these dates, which has greatly affected people's lives. There were no mysteries around Elizabeth Bell – she spoke as she found, plain and simple, always with compassion, always with a helping hand. To say she will be deeply missed would be an understatement.

Tim and his parents stayed at Grandma's cottage for the funeral. Aunty Anne and Rebecca, who'd arrived the previous day, had booked a room at the George and Dragon. Aunty Anne had been busy sorting things out, so the cottage was clean and tidy, though some things had been moved and some seemed to be missing. In some way, it felt as if Grandma was still there, not only in their memories. At times they almost expected to hear echoes of her voice.

Many local people, young and old alike, had turned out to say their goodbyes. Life moves in circles. Times were changing, and the next generation was now being called upon to take the place of the old. Before long, it would be the turn of Tim's generation.

At the end of the service, the people rose to sing one of grandma's favourites, Psalm 23, 'The Lord is my shepherd I shall not want.' Tim and the other pallbearers took their places beside the coffin, and on the instructions of the funeral directors, they hoisted it up onto their shoulders and walked steadily up the aisle. Others joined them, and the procession moved slowly to the back of the church. At the entrance porch, they turned right and, keeping to the same slow pace, continued past headstones that spanned many centuries. The funeral directors took over at the graveside and laid the coffin across the open grave on two planks. The priest spoke words, and final prayers were said as the coffin was lowered. Family and friends solemnly scattered handfuls of soil into the grave.

Grandma would have approved of the sandwiches, cakes and drinks served up in the little hall that day, homemade by women of the village, under the guidance of Mrs Baker, of course.

Joining Uncle Bill, Tim asked how he was.

"I'll be all right. It was a shock, of course, though I was pleased to be with her when she passed. She was so peaceful."

Tim wanted to change the subject and was keen to know if Bill still visited the stones and how they seemed these days.

"Oh aye, I often walk that way. Do you know, they look better than I can ever remember. This sounds daft, but it's as if they have new life. But for those stones, none of us would be here."

The Inner Circle

He was right, for the villages followed on from that ancient settlement.

"I like to go to the inner circle too," Tim replied. "I know that after I spent time alone there, all my worries and thoughts have become hopes and dreams."

"That's a great philosophy. You're growing into a fine young man. Despite all that nonsense I used to tell you."

They laughed and chatted for a while longer, and then Tim said he needed some fresh air and would take a walk to the standing stones. Pulling up his coat collar, he set out along the lane, hands sunk in his pockets. When he was still a few hundred yards off the stones, he stopped, sensing an energy, an excitement, and the memories flooded in – the memories of that day when the entire world shook. Then, returning to the present, he walked the last few yards, entered the stone circle, and sat down in the centre.

"Thank you, Grandma, for all you gave us. Rest in peace, knowing that your love will last for eternity. We'll take care of everything exactly as you would wish."

Tim took leave of the circle as he'd always done, walking clockwise, touching each stone in turn. Stones whose shapes were rough yet smooth to the touch. The sun was dipping over the hills now, and it was time to head back to the family for one last formality – the reading of the will.

Inheritance

Returning to the little hall, the will reading took place that evening. True to her nature, Grandma had written names underneath or on the backs of furniture, pictures, and other ornaments, ready for their new owners. It was as if she had known her time was close. Grandma had put Tim down as Timothy Walker, but then in brackets, *Timmy Flea*. Which sounded strange now, but then it reminded him that Timmy Flea was still very much part of him.

The solicitor only had to read out Grandma's instructions, and when he did, Tim was amazed to learn she'd left him her cottage, to do with as he saw fit. When all the documents and keys were placed in his hands, his dad reassured him that he was there to help with this new responsibility. Grandma's considerable savings were to be split between other close family members. There'd been no mention of a walking stick, Tim noticed. Presumably, that would still be at the cottage.

Later that evening, all the family and friends gathered at the George and Dragon, where, for the first time in many years, every one of their Bed & Breakfast rooms was fully booked. Even though people were tired, all they wanted to do was talk, so the event seemed to go on forever. Tim was asked what he would do with the cottage. Would he move in and live there? But still surprised by Grandma's bequest, he told them he would have to wait and see.

His heart sank when Rebecca entered the room with the stick in her hand. She walked over and handed it to him. "This had your name on it, and I wanted to be the one to bring it to you."

Holding the stick gently in his hand, Tim smiled. "I know you wanted this stick when we were young." They looked at each other and recognised a common bond for the first time.

"I always wanted everything, didn't I? Mainly because I knew my mother would buy me anything I wanted. Now I know, only to seek the things that I need, important things." Reaching for Tim's hand, Rebecca gave it a firm squeeze. "I'm going to miss Grandma," she said.

Tim hugged her without thinking. "You can use the cottage whenever you like. I can't see myself living here and working away. But I can't think of selling it either."

"Oh, I found this too." Rebecca reached into her bag and handed him an envelope with his name on it. "It looks like it was just waiting for a stamp."

Opening it, he found a note in Grandma's writing and a playing card. He read the words, *found this, and thought of you.* The card, of course, was a Joker. *You seem to have gained so much in so little time.* Grandma had continued. *All the suits are yours. Hearts, Spades, Diamonds, and Clubs. You are truly a wild card, which can be used in many ways.*

After eleven, people began to leave, and the Walker family could return to the cottage. With Origen in one hand, Tim opened the door with his new key and stepped over the threshold. It was not long before his parents went to bed, but Tim sat for a while in grandma's old chair. The cottage was in darkness, but he was not afraid. "It's been a long-time, Stick, yet it seems like only yesterday."

"Yes, Tim, you have travelled far, but much more is yet to come."

Closing his eyes, Tim let out a long breath. "I am beginning to know who I am now. Timmy Flea still, but known as Tim. I'm no longer afraid and can stand my ground, so surely nothing is impossible."

"*Getting to know ourselves is an ongoing process,*" Origen continued. "*As you journey on, more things will become visible. Though strangely, as you grow, you begin to see how small you are compared to all there is. Then one day, the big realisation dawns. You are one with nature and the whole universe. Remember how that feels when you relax and find peace, as you become one with everything.*"

"I guess so, but what am I to do with it all, this being one?" Tim asked. "There are so many divisions in this world. It's not easy, and it's not perfect. Not by a long way."

"*That is life's challenge, Tim. For someone to know that things can be better, living as one with all things – at the same time, to be able to dwell in our broken world. The solution is to begin with yourself. Resolve your fears, anger, guilt, and beliefs that limit your possibilities. Discover your oneness with the universe, and you will find peace flows from you, accepting differences, valuing others in their many similarities.*"

In the background was the reassuring sound of the kitchen clock as Origen continued, "*It's important to recognise that oneness with the universe and all that it holds, nature and all of humanity is not just a nice peaceful feeling, It's an active way of life towards all things. Everything exists within you – this is where you began. Your inner self is like a castle to be explored. Discovering that you are one with everything outside you is like an awakening. In every heart, there is a place of infinite longing for oneness, and the experience of peaceful oneness motivates us to this way of living. We allow a moment to happen when the sensing mind* quiets and overtakes the thinking mind. I believe that under such conditions, it's relatively easy to forget the self and instead become so wrapped up in sensing that paradoxically you, the sensor, disappear into the sensuous world of nature. Often, people who search for oneness chase after the experience of that peaceful moment, which is good. However, they can miss the whole point – that our broken world can be healed through living the way of oneness. A way of life that accepts the differences of others, shows empathy and compassion and recognises that all manner of things can be achieved together. The world encourages separateness as the only way – this works against our natural laws and destroys rather than creates harmony, peace, and mutual understanding. This is the true way of life fashioned by the Master Magician. These are the doors through which we enter a universe of infinite possibilities."

It had been a long day and Tim headed to his small bedroom. He hung the stick on the hook behind the door and tucked down to sleep. Inheritance, he thought, seems to be more about responsibility and carrying things on than it did ownership.

The Dragon

For Tim, no day was ordinary. Each one brought something new, and he was never bored. He was even beginning to succeed at using his imagination to centre his mind on peace and tranquility.

Tim's first visit to the cottage as its new owner took place only a few weeks after Grandma's funeral. He'd recently passed his driving test, so, borrowing his dad's car, he drove there alone. The journey went well, and, quite proud of himself, he rang home to let his folks know he'd arrived safely.

It didn't take him long to settle in. Having stocked the fridge and cupboards with some basic supplies and prepared a meal for later, he went upstairs. First, he set up the camp bed, which he now swore was more comfortable than a regular one. Then, thinking they were well overdue a catchup, he brought down the walking stick. Finally, with a small table of food next to him and the stick on his lap, he settled down in the armchair.

"I've been thinking," Tim began, "was there really a dragon in Rune Hill, and if so, what happened to him after the stone was taken?"

"*There was certainly a dragon, but he may not be aware that the gemstone he guarded has gone or that the Dark Man hid it within his darkness. He may well be chasing every shadow still. People are the same – sometimes they don't realise they are free, that neither bars nor locked doors imprison them, only their thoughts.*"

Tim hesitated. "What if I were to tell that dragon he is free to go – would that be very dangerous, do you think?"

"*If you're truly motivated by a desire to set the dragon free, it should be safe enough.*"

Tim thought about this. "But what would the world be like with a dragon on the loose? Might it be better to leave well alone?"

"*There isn't a yes or no answer,*" Origen said. "*I can see the consequences of both, but you must choose where your heart leads you.*"

Tim slept on this idea, though in his heart, he knew he had already decided.

After breakfast the following day, Tim set out. It was misty when he headed towards Rune Hill, walking stick in hand. He had butterflies in his stomach, but the journey was nowhere as fraught as last time.

"Can all dragons fly?" Tim asked after a time.

"*Many of them can, but not all,*" Origen replied. "*It depends on their specific powers. This one will certainly be able to move from one place to another, but I wouldn't worry about that too much.*"

"Do I need to leave you outside the cave again?"

"*Yes, I am afraid you do.*"

Tim recognised the cave entrance at once. At this time of the morning, there was not a soul about, but he took care to leave Origen in a safe place. Remembering last time, Tim had brought a powerful torch and a piece of chalk to mark the walls. He also recalled how cold it was there, so had brought a warm jacket. As he walked deeper into the cave, he wondered exactly how one attracted a dragon's attention. After about half an hour, he heard a snorting noise. It sounded uncomfortably like a warning. Tim was terrified. Nevertheless, he said, "My name is Tim, and I want to help you leave this cave."

When the dragon finally revealed himself, Tim gasped. "You're much smaller than I expected."

"Oh? So how many dragons have *you* met?"

"Um... Anyway, I've come to tell you that you no longer have any reason to stay here. You're free to go."

The dragon snorted. "You're quite wrong. A magician summoned me and bound me under a spell to protect the stone, which is a task I've fulfilled for many years. Even when the Dark Man deceived me and hid the stone, I knew he was under a spell himself – the spell of greed. I knew he could never leave the cave with that stone. So, you see, I've been a prisoner here for over four hundred years and must remain for many more."

"No. The stone really has gone. The spell's broken and you can go free."

The dragon laughed. "What do *you* know? You're not a magician."

"I always speak the truth, and it is the truth that will set you free."

"Hmm, you do sound an honest person and speak with some authority. How did the stone go?"

"I took the stone, the Dark Man has gone, and the stone was placed back with the other eight. There was an earthquake, and all were buried. The stone circle and time are safe."

The dragon flexed his wings. "Very well, let us head for the outside world, then we will see."

"But what if someone sees you?"

"No problem. I can detect human presence in the dark, and once I'm out in the light of day, my powers of invisibility will be restored, and I can fly unseen to the Land of the Dragons – if what you say is true."

They reached the cave entrance. And after a pause, the dragon looked around and said, "To demonstrate my gratitude, I will grant you a wish. What will it be? Wealth? Health? Love perhaps?"

Tim thought for a moment, and then he said, "I'd

like to know how I can always do the right thing, please."

"So be it," the dragon said, placing a claw gently on Tim's shoulder. "Now close your eyes," he instructed as they emerged into the light. "This," he said, spreading wide his mighty wings so the scales glittered in the sun, "may make some dust."

Eyes tight shut, Tim heard powerful wingbeats, and when he opened them again, he was just in time to see the dragon launch himself into the air. The next moment he'd vanished, and all Tim could make out were faint ripples in the mist, which receded into the far distance, and then were gone. Turning away, he collected Origen, and as they made their way slowly back to the cottage, Tim told the stick everything that had happened in the cave.

"*So, Tim, you speak to dragons and set them free now,*" Origen said. "*Whatever will you do next?*"

The Inner Circle

The Inner Circle

Hearts Clubs Diamonds Spades

Tim had reached the ripe old age of thirty-six, and one Saturday afternoon, he was in the city centre, looking to buy a pair of shoes. His quest was interrupted by a torrential downpour, so he ran for shelter in the nearest building, which happened to be the old library. The sudden change from the noise of rain and people rushing to the stillness of the library was such a contrast that it took him a moment to adjust to it. He had no idea where he was going in this vast building, but he was aware of people looking at him and that he had burst in there, disturbing their silence. Tiptoeing to a side aisle, he found himself surrounded by shelves of books, old and new. Reaching a staircase to the upper gallery and reference section, he went on up. He had not been there for a long time, yet the smell of wood polish, leather and paper had not changed.

Running his fingers along the book spines, Tim suddenly wanted to turn their pages. He stopped for no specific reason, resting his hand on a small leather-bound book. He saw it was decorated with hearts, spades, diamonds, and clubs and read the title, *Playing Cards*. Finding a spot to sit, he began to explore the book. There were so many things he had not known. Hearts signify water, Spades belong to the air, Diamonds are of the earth, and Clubs indicate fire. Shouldn't there be a Joker, though, Tim wondered, recalling times when the family played cards at the cottage. He turned to the index and was directed to page 132 – the Joker.

As he read further, Tim was struck by the Joker's similarity to Jack – he too concealed his wisdom behind his foolish appearance and behaviour, displaying opposite or distorted messages to all but the wise. The Joker, surrounded by ancient symbols, is powerful, mysterious, and unpredictable. Tim pondered on whether this book found him and, if so, why? What was he meant to do with this knowledge? Should he create a new game, complete with rules? After a while, Tim began to feel a close bond with the Joker and his inclusive nature. The symbolism of the Joker card illuminated Tim's own identity, revealing an energy, skill, and power he was previously unaware of. Recognising and taking on the character of the Joker, Tim stepped forward in his power and completeness.

He appeared from the library and realised he had taken longer than he intended, so decided to take the shorter route home, down by the river, through streets daubed with graffiti tags. This was a deprived area, often avoided by city dwellers. It was also controlled by two gangs, the *East Hill Mob* and *Blade*. Both locked in a perpetual war over territory, drug dealing, and protection rackets. Any interaction between Blade and Mob members would create verbal abuse or worse. No gang member dared enter another's area. These territorial wars could never be won but needed to be continually defended, so the hatred and rivalry persisted. These were two organised crime groups with no respect for anyone but themselves. Violence was commonplace, and over the last twenty years, at least three lives had been lost. Blade, who considered themselves outsiders, had created a lifestyle financed by drug dealing. At the same time, the East Hill Mob was dominated by a Mafia-style family, their protection racket underpinned by a reign of terror. The gangs' disputes might have been over business, but the hatred was personal, and survival depended on strict segregation.

As Tim turned into Watland Road, he headed towards an underpass beneath the high-level motorway, which crossed the river and cut through the city. Two young men, probably no more than twenty years old, were in a stand-off. Steve, a high-ranking member of the East Hill Mob, and Isaac, from the Blade gang. Steve held a knife, as Isaac fearlessly hurled abuse. The pair seemed intent on settling the feud, one way or another.

As Tim drew closer, rational thought was cast aside and he felt compelled to step into the situation. Isaac, the taller, heavier-built youth, continued his verbal tirade, and Steve, head-shaven, and covered in tattoos, menacingly flayed his knife around. Tim was clear in his mind for the first time in his life about what would happen next. "Oi... Stop that now," he shouted.

Shocked that anyone dared speak to gang members like this, they stopped at once, and two pairs of eyes turned towards him.

Steve reacted first. "No, you stop. Turn around and leave. This is none of your business." Tim continued to go closer, almost within arm's length.

Isaac sneered. "Yeah, clear off. You got a death wish or something?"

"Nobody needs to die today," Tim replied, showing his open hands. This was not something Steve or Isaac were used to, as their instinct was to strike first. Steve was still waving the knife around in small circles, then with a quick haymaker, he slashed Tim's right cheek, drawing blood. Tim held his ground.

"He's crazy," Steve said.

It wasn't a deep cut, and Tim paid no attention to it. Instead, spreading his arms in a cruciform position with palms upright, he told them, "I want you to see what I can see. Put your hands in my hands if you are brave enough."

The Inner Circle

The pair glanced at each other and frowned but were drawn to play along in this strange game. Isaac placed his right hand into Tim's left, and then Steve put his left hand into Tim's right, still holding the knife between him and Isaac. Tim closed his grip, and both Steve and Isaac flinched.

"There's nothing to fear. It's like watching a movie." Tim spoke in the language of the stick. Not something he had intended. It simply happened. The world for them turned black, and images and sounds of war and suffering appeared in slow motion, expanding an emotional connection. Isaac and Steve were shaking but could not let go, and the knife fell to the ground. The horror of what humanity can do to his fellow man became a vivid truth.

As the intensity increased, there was a sudden shift to peace and light. There became a vision of nature in all its glory. A pattern was forming around nature's oneness and our interconnection with each other. Differences became less important as firm similarities appeared. Change was in motion as fear, guilt, and anger fell to the ground. It was replaced by forgiveness, acceptance, trust, and that word not often used in its true context – love.

Tim could see change as their faces softened and tense bodies relaxed. Isaac and Steve had not realised until now that they had linked their loose arms, completing the circle. Here was a new power they had not experienced before. Both opened their eyes to each other and said, "This has to stop. We are brothers." Tim released his hold – the cut on his cheek had healed.

Tim continued, "The statement, we never learn, is not true. We do learn, but we must put our learning into practice. Take down the barricades that have been built and build on relationships of mutual respect. There is far more similarity about you than differences."

He had no idea where this had come from, and he was also shaking a little too. No one was there to see this, and no one would ever know. These rivals had become brothers, and life would be different. Steve and Isaac sat down together and planned how they would speak to the other gang members. Meanwhile, Tim slipped out of sight.

The Inner Circle

Letting go

In the next two years, something significant happened to Tim. He met Ann at a pub quiz night and found they were soulmates. Before long, they fell in love, and one Sunday afternoon, while walking by the river, Tim proposed marriage. His mum was not surprised, though his dad didn't see it coming. They were married in the summer of 2005 and moved into a small apartment not far from Tim's parents.

Though the couple were married late in life, they hoped for children. Sadly, this was not to be, though a golden retriever named Hudson went part of the way in filling that gap. Tim was promoted to assistant warehouse manager, and Ann worked as a teaching assistant. They had some savings, but the cost of buying a house with a garden seemed out of their reach.

Over the next few years, they saved and took simple holidays at the cottage. As both Tim and Ann's parents were getting old and would need their care, the logical choice would be to sell the cottage and buy a house just outside the city. Tim approached his parents for their thoughts, and the decision was made. Grandma's cottage would be sold.

Tim and Ann were busy at work during one of a few trips to complete minor repairs and to give the cottage a lick of paint.

There was a knock at the door. "I'll get it," Ann said as Tim was up a ladder. She opened the door to an impeccably dressed man in tweed.

"I would like to speak to Tim. Is he here?"

"It's someone for you," Ann said, leaving the man

standing in the doorway. Tim wiped his hands and straightened his clothes. His heart sank as he saw Luke Crozier.

"Hello, Tim, I heard you were selling the cottage. Thought I would add it to my estate, and as you and I are friends, I thought we could do a deal."

The pair had parted on reasonable terms, but Tim still didn't trust him. "Sorry, Luke, it's going to auction. There's a lot of interest in it."

"I am sure we can come to an arrangement," Luke insisted. "You must have a price in mind, come on, what do you say?"

Ann, standing behind Tim, had no prior knowledge of Luke or any of Tim's early life experiences, but as Tim's feet were firmly placed on the threshold, it was clear Luke was not welcome, nor was his offer.

Tim folded his arms. "I have a contract with the Estate Agents and the Auction house. It's out of my hands. So best you leave now."

Luke frowned. "I'll see you on the day of the auction. I will have this property." And with that, he left.

Tim's heart pounded. The last thing he wanted was for a Crozier to own Grandma's cottage. Ann put her arms around his waist and hugged him from behind. "It'll be okay, Tim, you'll see."

The pair got on with their tasks, and soon the tiny cottage was in good to fair condition. Tim had promised Grandma he would take care of everything, so furniture and oddments had been sold or gifted, and items of sentimental value had been boxed and stored away until Tim could find new space for them.

The day for handing over the keys to the Estate agent arrived. The auction was the following day, so Ann and Tim stayed at the George and Dragon that night. On auction day, the room was packed, though it was difficult to know who had come with the intent to buy and how many were just plain nosey. Tim kept looking around. This had been the hardest decision for him, though he knew it was right.

Ann gave his hand a reassuring squeeze. "Soon be done now, Tim," she said.

The auctioneer called the room to order and began to describe Grandma's cottage. At that, the main door banged shut, and Tim swung round to see Luke enter the room and stand by a side pillar. The bidding started and rose quickly to a respectable amount, after which it increased slowly in increments of £500. Then Luke entered the bidding, calling out a figure of £1500 ahead of the last bit. The room fell silent. Then another £500 bid came over the telephone. Everyone else had dropped out, so it was between Luke and the telephone bidder. Luke's voice faltered as he called out his next bid. The telephone bidder replied with £2,000 ahead of his bid. Luke, stormed out of the room, muttering under his breath.

"I'm pleased about that," Tim told Ann. "Not because we got more than we expected, but that Luke Crozier didn't get the cottage. I wonder who the new owner is?"

Tim and Ann went to the office to complete the transaction. "Are you able to tell us who the buyer is?" Tim asked.

"Sorry, confidentiality. I'm sure they'll be in touch with you before long."

Both were puzzled but left happy that they could begin to look for their new home. They travelled back to the city that night, and the following day there was a phone call.

"Hi, it's Rebecca. How are you both? I've not seen you in a long time."

"We are fine, thanks. The cottage has gone." Tim had a lump in his throat. "Sorry. We all have good memories of it and our times there together."

"And will have," Rebecca said with a giggle.

"What do you mean?"

"I bought it, of course, so it's still in the family. I have the money, and it just felt right."

Tim, lost for words, indicated to Ann what had happened.

"Now, you two, get on and find your dream house with a garden. I'll catch up with you in a few weeks."

Within six months, Tim, Ann, and Hudson the dog had moved into their new house. It had the garden they wanted, and there was an attic room where Tim could store all those special things from Grandma's cottage, including his grandad's drawings. Behind the door to the loft, he fastened a hook so the stick could hang there, while a good light from the large window enabled him to sketch, regaining his youthful passion.

Origen

Time continued at its regular speed, but things seemed to be much slower for Tim and Ann. Tim had been made manager at the warehouse and was now addressed as Mr Walker. They kept in contact with Rebecca and often visited the cottage. So, when she rang asking if they would come the following weekend, they said, "Yes, of course, we will."

Tim had spent time in the attic room, completing a large sketch of the stone circle. His thoughts returned to his teenage years and his great adventure there. He glanced at the stick hanging on the door and wondered what would become of it. It could stay there forever, of course, though someone will move it eventually. He used the word stick rather than Origen, keeping emotion and practical decision-making separate.

Should he give the stick to someone, but who could he give it to? Grandma gave him the stick, though without knowing what she was giving. Tim could sell it or give it to a charity shop. Whoever the stick ended up with, it might choose not to speak to them. All of that was beyond Tim's control. What if he just left it somewhere for another person to find?

In the action of letting go, you had to be content with your decision, happy to let go with your hands and your heart. Perhaps that time had come.

They were about to set off to the cottage, and Ann was waiting at the car, with Hudson on the back seat. "Have you got *everything* now?" she said with a hint of sarcasm. Tim would always take more bits and bobs with him than he needed.

"Just about done. I thought I would take Grandad's

old stick."

"You planning to do some walking then?"

Tim hesitated before continuing, "Well, we'll see. I might take Hudson through the woods. Come on, we will never get there at this rate."

Ann laughed. "I'll drive."

Once at the cottage, Ann helped Rebecca in the kitchen while Tim unpacked.

Rebecca glanced at the stick in Tim's hand. "I haven't seen that for a while. I'd forgotten about it. Leave it in the corner and come and eat. All is prepared."

The cottage had modernisations carried out recently, which had not spoilt its character. "I like what you've done to the place," Tim remarked. "It looks loved."

"I have the work done while I am not around and I think the workmen prefer it that way. Do let me know if you want a week here on your own, won't you?"

Rebecca carried the stick through when they settled in the living room after tea. "So, Tim, what's the story about this stick?"

Tim looked at the stick and was about to speak when Ann interrupted. "Well, it's just an old stick, once owned by your grandad. Isn't that right, Tim?"

"Well, yes and no, really," Tim stammered. But Rebecca would not let this go, and Tim knew it.

"Come on, Tim, spill the beans, old man."

Tim laughed. There were just three years between them. "Old man indeed," he said. "It's special because our grandad carved the head and the words running down the shaft."

Rebecca examined the stick. "I never knew that. Well, I never. Hold on to what you have." She ran her finger over the words. "I guess the biggest part is *knowing* what we have."

"I will tell you the whole story – of a stick called Origen," he said as he curled his feet up in the armchair.

The Inner Circle

"Providing you promise this will stay within these walls."

Rebecca's eyes widened. "Oh, we promise, don't we, Ann? Hang on while I get some drinks. This sounds like it will take a while."

They were both agog. Even Hudson had one ear raised. "It's probably best to listen and save any questions until the end," Tim said and they all nodded in agreement. "I met Origen thirty-two years ago. He was carved and named by Grandad. As I rested by the waterfall, he spoke to me and what followed was the most amazing adventure." Tim told of Halvor the wizard, Dragon hill and all about the stone circle and the castle. Later he described how he had met Luke Crozier and seen the hidden chamber, how he decided that the missing stone was the link to the crumbling stone circle and the legend of the collapse of time. His account of how he came up against darkness in the cave and took the crystal stone had the girls on tenterhooks. When the stone was replaced, an earthquake shook the area, and the castle turret collapsed. He noted how Jack and the wind were always around, and the Joker played his part too.

Some parts were omitted – the journey to the centre of the universe, the vision of Peter in the stone circle, and the episode between Steve and Isaac.

"This has to be true," Ann said. "You could never have made all this up. And I see it in all your drawings too."

Rebecca was speechless. This was a first for her, then asked, "I don't know what to think. Will Origen speak to us?"

"We could try," he said. "We'll take hold of the stick, all of us together, and close your eyes. I don't know why I said that. I am sure it doesn't make any difference."

Rebecca held the head, Ann held the other end, and Tim had the middle in both hands. Nothing happened -- no voice and no sound. But that was the thing. There was no sound at all. It was as if everything had stopped. Each one stared at the other. They knew something strange was happening. There was no sense of fear, only peace. Then Origen spoke softly.

"The magic is not in me. It is in each of you. Keep going forward and see how much you can achieve. Remember the words of Halvor. 'Be aware of the Puppet Master.' Now, you no longer need me. You have everything you need."

At that, normal sounds returned to the room. The three of them stood in amazement.

"It's true," Tim said. "There is much more around us than we ever realise."

"It's like the Wizard of Oz. We will all wake up soon," Rebecca said. "But I know I'm fully awake now – more than I have ever been. You're right, Tim. This stays with us or people would say we are crazy."

The story had taken all evening, and it was time to retire to bed. Tim decided to set his alarm early for the following day. There was another task to be done.

New Roots

Tim got up as quietly as possible, picked up the stick and headed to the front door. Hudson was not going to pass up on a walk and began to make a fuss of him. Tim spoke softly, "Okay, you can come too. But best behaviour."

They headed towards the woods, Tim holding Origen firmly in his hand and the leather strap around his wrist. Hudson followed close behind. The chatter of a jackdaw came from the tall trees, though this could not have been Jack after so many years.

Turning right, he headed towards Hollywell house and tried to find a way through. The paths were not as well used as they were, and nature was busy reclaiming them. Reaching the house, Tim smiled as he saw the jackdaw fly to the chimney top. He wondered how many generations had lived there.

Hudson was busy chasing the smell of squirrels. So, holding Origen close, Tim said, "The time has come to let you go, old friend."

Origen broke his silence. "*By letting go of me, I can be reborn, and there will be many more adventures to be had for both of us.*"

Tim kept things simple and didn't want to draw this out. "Thank you for being part of my journey." He swung the stick behind his shoulder and threw it with all his strength. He couldn't quite see where it landed but heard the sound as it broke through the bushes. Then, turning away, he walked on towards the waterfall.

Unbeknown to him, once he was a fair distance away, a jackdaw flew down to where the stick had landed. The bird began scratching at the ground, and before long, the stick was buried in rich soil close to a trickle of water from the spring. In years to come, a new ash tree would grow up out of this very spot.

Tim headed towards the waterfall, the place where it all began. It was easy for him to imagine his younger self sitting against the tree with Origen, chatting away about the nature of things. That had been the strangest of days and only the beginning of great discoveries. Without thinking, he called out, "You're going to be just fine, Timmy Flea. Just fine."

Thoughts drifted through his mind like a river flowing ever onward. "Not to worry, not to stress. All things will pass, and I will remain, knowing who I am, a better person for seeing things in a different light. All is one with the world. All is well. Life is a journey, and we do not always have a map. It's not the road we choose that's important but how we travel that road and the things we learn as we go. It would have been much easier if I'd had a route map with all the right turns to follow. But I would have missed out on the adventure."

It was still early, and Tim didn't expect anyone to be awake at the cottage. He continued up and out of the wood and then towards the stone circle. As it came into view, Hudson barked and ran on ahead. A figure was sitting in the middle, face lifted to the sunrise. It was Ann – she stood up and turned to meet Hudson. "Hey, you. Have you been out for an early walk?"

Tim came up and they hugged. "Morning," Tim said. "I didn't want to wake you."

"You didn't. I guessed where you would be when I woke up and thought I'd join you." The pair sat on the grass, back-to-back, propping each other up, Tim's left hand holding her right. "It's so beautiful here. I can see why you love it."

"He's gone. Origen. I let him go. There was no need to hold on to him any longer. I returned him to nature. It seemed the right thing to do."

Ann squeezed his hand. "I do love you." Then she pointed and said, "Is that your jackdaw, up there on the tallest stone? He seems to be watching us."

Tim stood up, raised his arm, and said, "Come on, Jack, come to me." At once, the bird opened its wings, and he flew down onto Tim's sleeve. This intimate moment did not last long, as one very jealous dog, Hudson, jumped up and barked loudly. "I was just a boy the first time that happened. But I remember it was like being touched by magic. Young Timmy Flea is still here."

Back at the cottage, they began to prepare breakfast, and Rebecca woke to the smell of fried bacon. "Morning. You two are up early."

"We've been for a walk," Ann said. "It's going to be a lovely day, a shame to be going home."

"You know you are welcome anytime. I say, that smells good. Shall we eat?"

Sitting around the table, Tim explained why he had been out early. Ann thought he had done the right thing, but Rebecca was disappointed. She'd wanted the experience of talking with Origen. Nevertheless, she respected Tim's action. Life surely would be different, having access to magic.

Once they were back home, Tim completed the drawing of the stone circle. In the centre, he drew two figures sitting back-to-back. Ann loved this image and she had it framed and hung in their front room, pride of place.

Timmy Flea and Tim had become one and the same. A warrior who had followed a hero's journey. Doubts, hesitation, and fears had tried to hold him back. His mentor Origen arrived when Timmy was at a low ebb. In the face of all opposition, he had been encouraged by Halvor and Jack on a quest whose purpose gradually became clear.

Changes were taking place on the inside, then becoming visible on the outside, just as with the chrysalis and the butterfly, when beauty and truth begin to appear.

Tim's true self and purpose in life had appeared and continued to grow.

So now – go and find the magic yourself.

The Inner Circle

Printed in Great Britain
by Amazon